P9-AQQ-004

"Firefighting is special. You make a real difference in the world."

Genuine admiration tinged Aubrey's voice, and his chest swelled.

"Like being a nurse?

"Firefighting is nothing like being a nurse. You put your life on the line for others. That takes courage and daring." She tilted her head and stared him square in the face. "I have to say, Gage, you really impress me. Not that I wasn't—"

She didn't have a chance to finish, because he hauled her into his arms, lifted her onto her toes and brought her mouth to within a tiny fraction of his.

Her green eyes went wide. "If you're thinking of kissing me, think again."

"Oh, I'm going to kiss you, all right."

Dear Reader,

Some years ago when my family was visiting Young, Arizona, I had the opportunity to meet the Payson Hotshots. The crew, fresh from the front line of the fire, strode into the Antler Café where we were having dinner, turning every head in the place. In speaking to them, we learned the citizens of Young were helping out by hosting the wilderness firefighters—feeding them and putting them up for the night at the local community center.

That weekend while I stood on our cabin porch watching the fire blaze in the nearby mountains, I wondered about the Hotshots and the amazing individuals who chose to work in such a dangerous profession. I also wondered about the people who loved them and made up their families.

From that experience, Gage and Aubrey's story was born. *His Only Wife* is my first Harlequin American Romance, a line that I'm thrilled to be writing for. I hope you enjoy reading about Gage and Aubrey as much as I enjoyed writing about them.

Warmest wishes,

Cathy McDavid

P.S. I love hearing from readers. Visit my Web site at www.cathymcdavid.com to drop me a line.

His Only Wife
CATHY McDAVID

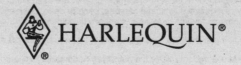

HARLEQUIN®

TORONTO • NEW YORK • LONDON
AMSTERDAM • PARIS • SYDNEY • HAMBURG
STOCKHOLM • ATHENS • TOKYO • MILAN • MADRID
PRAGUE • WARSAW • BUDAPEST • AUCKLAND

If you purchased this book without a cover you should be aware that this book is stolen property. It was reported as "unsold and destroyed" to the publisher, and neither the author nor the publisher has received any payment for this "stripped book."

ISBN-13: 978-0-373-75172-3
ISBN-10:   0-373-75172-9

HIS ONLY WIFE

Copyright © 2007 by Cathy McDavid.

All rights reserved. Except for use in any review, the reproduction or utilization of this work in whole or in part in any form by any electronic, mechanical or other means, now known or hereafter invented, including xerography, photocopying and recording, or in any information storage or retrieval system, is forbidden without the written permission of the publisher, Harlequin Enterprises Limited, 225 Duncan Mill Road, Don Mills, Ontario M3B 3K9, Canada.

This is a work of fiction. Names, characters, places and incidents are either the product of the author's imagination or are used fictitiously, and any resemblance to actual persons, living or dead, business establishments, events or locales is entirely coincidental.

This edition published by arrangement with Harlequin Books S.A.

® and TM are trademarks of the publisher. Trademarks indicated with ® are registered in the United States Patent and Trademark Office, the Canadian Trade Marks Office and in other countries.

www.eHarlequin.com

Printed in U.S.A.

ABOUT THE AUTHOR

For the past eleven years Cathy McDavid has been juggling a family, a job, and writing and doing pretty well at it except for the cooking and housecleaning part. Mother of boy and girl teenage twins, she manages the near impossible by working every day with her husband of twenty years at their commercial construction company. They survive by not bringing work home and not bringing home to the office. A mutual love of all things Western also helps. Horses and ranch animals have been a part of Cathy's life since she moved to Arizona as a child and asked her mother for riding lessons. She can hardly remember a time when she couldn't walk outside and pet a soft, velvety nose (or beak, or snout) whenever the mood struck.

This book is dedicated to the courageous men and women who serve as wilderness firefighters in the western United States and all over the world. It has been a joy writing about you and an honor to make your acquaintance.

Chapter One

Tourists in motor homes, cowboys in pickup trucks, and teenagers in hot rods with the radios blasting.

Not much had changed about the Pineville service station over the last decade from what Aubrey Stuart could see, except maybe the price of gas.

And her.

She guided her mini SUV toward the far island and parked beside a pump. Pushing the door open with one hand, she grabbed her tiny purse off the front passenger seat and stepped outside. In the blink of an eye, she exchanged air-conditioned comfort for the heat of Arizona high country in late June.

While waiting for her credit card purchase to be authorized, she removed the cap from her gas tank and eyed the constant stream of vehicles coming and going. Everything about this place was familiar to Aubrey. During the four-hour drive from Tucson, she'd steeled herself against the pain that the sight of Pineville always brought on during those few short visits she'd made through the years. But to her vast relief, there wasn't any. Only a twinge of melancholy.

Could it be she was really and truly over Gage Raintree?

A high-pitched electronic beep drew her attention to the gas pump and the message scrolling across the panel in vivid green letters.

"Cash only, 'see clerk inside," Aubrey read out loud and sighed. With another hour's drive still ahead of her, she had wanted this to be a quick in-and-out stop.

Better to be safe than sorry, she decided. Thirty-foot drop-offs in some places made the winding dirt road to her grand-mother's home in Blue Ridge treacherous. Running out of gas halfway there would be at best an inconvenience, at worse a disaster.

Slamming the door of her SUV shut, she headed toward the minimart, extracting a twenty-dollar bill from her purse as she went. Ten years earlier, on the day she left Blue Ridge, she'd walked through this same door. In some ways, it felt like a lifetime ago. In other ways, only yesterday.

Back then, she'd been all innocence, painfully shy, and skinny as a broomstick. The brainy older daughter of renowned heart surgeon Alexander Stuart. Her younger sister, Annie, used to call her a nerd, and rightfully so. Aubrey hadn't just fit the description, she'd defined it. With the exception of Gage Raintree, the male population at large hardly noticed she existed.

"Enough already," she grumbled, snapping out of her reverie. An hour away from Blue Ridge and already she had a bad case of Gage Raintree on the brain. What would it be like when she arrived at her grandmother's?

Her movements purposeful, Aubrey strode into the mini-mart and went straight to stand in line behind several other people. The store was packed, taxing the sole clerk's limited abilities. She felt sorry for the poor kid when the man ahead of her vehemently complained about the inconvenience.

Her turn finally came. "Twenty dollars on pump three." She smiled pleasantly, handing the clerk her money. "And I need a receipt, please."

He appeared grateful that she wasn't going to bite his head off like everyone else. "Anything else, ma'am?"

"No, thank you." She took the receipt and started toward the door. At the sound of a familiar voice, her knees locked.

"Aubrey?"

She stood immobile and willed her gaze not to fly around the store.

"Aubrey, is that you?"

What were the odds of him being here? In this convenience store, at the exact same moment as her? Well, this was the last gas station on the road out of town.

"Aubrey Stuart?" the voice called again.

She had to look. There was simply no avoiding it. And, well, he didn't sound mad. That was a good sign, right? Mustering her courage, she turned slowly around and came face-to-face with her ex-husband.

"I thought you weren't arriving until tomorrow," he said.

"Hello, Gage." Her voice quivered. It had a tendency to do that when she was nervous or uncomfortable or, like now, both. "How are you?"

"Good. How 'bout yourself?" He moved ahead in line, closing the distance between them. "You look great."

His lingering appraisal of her appearance caused Aubrey's cheeks to heat. Never was she more aware of the fact that her younger, stick-figure self had filled out in all the right places.

"So do you," she blurted. "Look great, that is."

Of all things to gush forth from between her lips. Complete mental dysfunction was her only excuse. Gage did that to her. He always had.

But, sweet heaven, he did look great.

Tall to start with, he'd outgrown his once lanky form. There was no shortage of muscles bunching beneath his T-shirt. He wore his nearly black hair shorter than before. The wavy ends poked out from beneath his weathered cowboy hat to curl attractively at the base of his neck. His boots were scruffy, as always, and he needed a shave. Not that the dark stubble shadowing his jaw detracted from his good looks. Quite the contrary.

Rather than risk another embarrassing blunder, she forced her stiff legs to take a step toward the double glass doors at the front of the store. She'd known seeing him again would be a bit awkward, but she hadn't expected it to be so…disconcerting. "Guess I'll see you around."

"Hold up." He retrieved his change and plastic sack containing his purchases. "I'll walk you to your car."

"No!" At his bemused expression, she checked herself. "That's not necessary. You're obviously in a hurry."

"Actually, I'm not."

The sexy half smile he turned on her was potent as ever. Hoping to minimize its effects, she grabbed for the door handle nearest her and yanked, almost tearing her hand off in the process. The door rattled, but didn't open. Too late, she realized she'd pulled instead of pushed. Gage came up behind her, reached around and braced his hand on the glass panel near her head.

"Here. Let me get that for you." The door swung open, and a hot breeze struck Aubrey in the face.

She glanced over her shoulder. *Big* mistake.

His face hovered a few inches above hers. If she shifted slightly, she could find herself nestled in the crook of his arm. It was a place she'd been often enough as a teenager and remembered well.

A warning bell the size of Liberty herself rang inside Aubrey's head.

"Thanks." She shoved through the door and flashed him a smile she hoped radiated confidence. "See you around."

He followed, his long strides easily keeping pace with her. "Is this yours?" he asked when they reached her SUV.

"Mine and the bank's," she answered. Not wanting Gage to sense her discomfort, she made an effort to relax.

"Four-wheel drive. That'll come in handy around here." He gave the car the standard once-over typical of men, then hitched his chin at the neighboring island of gas pumps. "I'm still driving a pickup."

The long-bed crew cab he indicated was considerably newer and nicer than the one he'd driven in high school. And from what she could see, loaded to the hilt with lumber and various other building materials. He must have come into Pineville to purchase supplies for his family's cattle ranch. There was some sort of emblem on the driver-side door that she couldn't make out from this distance.

"It's big," she said and returned to filling her SUV with gas.

"I heard you were staying with your grandmother for a while. That's nice of you. A broken hip is no picnic, and I'm sure she appreciates your help."

"Yes." Small-town gossip, thought Aubrey. Nothing stayed secret for long. Everybody from the local sheriff to the clerk at the feed store had probably been informed of her arrival.

"Look, Aubrey," Gage said. "I know you probably feel a little…weird after what happened. Is there any chance we can get together and talk?"

"I'm not sure that's a good idea." She squeezed the gas nozzle until her fingers turned white. "I mean, what's to talk about? It was ages ago, and we've both moved on."

"But I don't want you feeling like you have to run for cover every time you see my pickup truck coming down the road. Blue Ridge is a small town. You can't walk across your front lawn without having to stop and chat with at least three people."

"I'm not going to run for cover every time I see you," she scoffed.

He gave her a skeptical look.

"Really." She hated that he knew her so well. But then, how could he not? They'd spent fifteen straight summers together, the last one as Mr. and Mrs. Raintree.

A loud click sounded, signaling her gas tank was full. Grateful for small favors, Aubrey jammed the nozzle back into the side of the pump. "I have to go. Grandma's expecting me." She slid in behind the wheel.

"Drive carefully. There's a lot of loose gravel on the roads." He shut her door for her.

Aubrey wiggled her fingers in farewell, then started the

SUV. Without meaning to, she sped out of the parking lot, succumbing to the urge to put as much distance between herself and Gage as possible.

Two miles outside of Pineville her heart rate finally dropped to double digits, and her breathing slowed. The worst was over, she told herself. She ran into Gage and had lived to tell about it. Next time wouldn't be so hard. Right?

Aubrey fervently hoped so. If not, this could be the longest six weeks of her life.

SOMETHING MUST HAVE happened. An accident maybe? Aubrey hit the brakes and came to a stop behind a Hummer hauling a trailer loaded with ATVs. She flipped up the sun visor and, squinting, stared out the windshield. For as far up the highway as she could see, traffic was at a standstill. It was then she realized there were no cars coming from the opposite direction.

After several minutes, people started getting out of their vehicles and milling around. Resigned to wait, Aubrey lowered her window and shut off her engine.

She didn't relish being stuck in a traffic jam, but at least she was safely away from Gage. Closing her eyes, she leaned back against the headrest and allowed the memories to come. Pain and hurt accompanied the steady stream of images filling her mind, convincing Aubrey that, despite her earlier conviction, she was anything but over Gage.

He'd been her first for many things. Her first kiss. Her first real date. Her first love. Her first—and only—husband. Without warning, her eyes began to tear.

"You okay?"

Aubrey sat bolt upright at the intrusion. A middle-aged man stood next to her open window.

"Ah…yeah," she mumbled, embarrassed at being caught on the verge of crying. "Just tired."

"I'm going down the line, passing the word. There's a wreck a mile or two up the road."

"Is it serious?"

"A semi and four cars, they're saying. Road's completely blocked in both directions."

The distant wail of a siren grew louder. As the ambulance passed, adrenaline flooded Aubrey's system, one of the many side effects of working in a hospital E.R., she supposed. Though, for her, it had recently become worse.

"Hope you brought a good book to read." The middle-aged man rapped her door and gave her a toothy smile before moving on. "We're gonna be here a while."

"Thanks," she called after him, her breathing, thankfully, slowing.

No book, but she had brought along some medical periodicals on health care for the aged and how to live independently after a hip fracture. She took one from the seat beside her and thumbed through it. Hopefully, she'd find something beneficial to her grandmother and compelling enough to keep her mind off the traffic jam. And Gage.

"Aubrey." He stood at her window.

Her hands involuntarily jerked, and the newsletter dropped onto her lap. "What are you doing here?"

"I'm about a dozen cars behind you. I walked up to check on you."

A dozen cars? He must have pulled out of the gas station right behind her.

"I'm fine." She collected the scattered newsletter pages.

"So we're back to that?"

"What?"

He leaned down and rested his forearms on her open window. "One- or two-word sentences."

Damn. He did know her well. "I guess."

His arms were tanned, the dusting of soft brown hair on them denser than she remembered. She shouldn't stare, but it was easier looking at his arms than his face.

"Is talking with me that tough?" he asked, readjusting his cowboy hat. "I remember when we'd stay up half the night talking. After we got married, we'd stay up half the night making l—"

"Details aren't necessary. I remember."

As did Gage, if his wide grin was any indication.

What was with him, anyway? They'd seen each other occasionally through the years, most recently at her grandfather's funeral. Those encounters had always been on the tense side and notably brief. Had enough time finally gone by that they could relax in each other's company and be themselves? It appeared so for Gage.

"Two whole sentences. That's a start." He chuckled and strode away.

But not to his truck. Instead, he cut behind her SUV and came up the passenger side. Before she could protest, he'd settled in beside her. Her glower had no dimming affects on the twinkle lighting his dark brown eyes.

"I don't remember inviting you in."

In response, he removed his cowboy hat and set it on the dash.

"Forget making yourself comfortable, you won't be staying long."

"Another thirty minutes, I'd say. The sheriff's office called in a special tow truck for the semi, and it hasn't arrived yet."

Siren wailing, the ambulance passed them going in the opposite direction toward Pineville. Momentarily distracted, Aubrey looked out her window. "I hope no one's injured."

"Two. Seriously, but not critically."

"How do you know all this?" She shot him a quizzical glance.

"I made a call on my cell phone. I have a friend who works in the newsroom at the radio station in Pineville."

"A friend?"

He turned toward her. "A *good* friend." His expression hinted at more.

"I'm happy for you." She crossed her arms over her middle and told herself it was indigestion and not jealousy gnawing at her stomach. For all she cared, he could have a thousand good friends.

"He and I went to fire academy together."

Aubrey groaned inwardly. Shame on her for walking right into his trap.

She remembered a very brief conversation they'd had at her grandfather's funeral when Gage mentioned joining the Blue Ridge Volunteer Fire Department. It was on the tip of her tongue to ask if he'd stuck with it, but she refrained, not certain she wanted to learn everything about him yet.

"You still a nurse in the emergency room at Tucson General?" He moved his seat back to accommodate his six-foot-plus frame.

Aubrey rolled her eyes and shook her head. The man had a lot of nerve. "Not at the moment."

"You quit your job?"

"I took a leave of absence."

"Wow." He stopped fiddling with the seat position and faced her. "I thought you loved nursing."

"I do." Aubrey heard her voice crack and swallowed before continuing. "Just not the E.R. lately."

She thought of Jesse and Maureen—saw them as she had at their thirtieth wedding anniversary, a hundred family members and friends in attendance to join them in celebrating. Dear friends of the Stuarts, Aubrey had known "Uncle" Jesse and "Aunt" Maureen practically her entire life. She remembered being deeply touched at the way they gazed sweetly into each other's faces. How wonderful it must be, she'd thought, to still be in love after so many years.

But then another, different image of Jesse's and Maureen's faces came to her. Broken and battered and covered in blood. Less than a week after the anniversary celebration, the couple had been brought into the E.R. while Aubrey was on duty, victims of an automobile accident. Upon glimpsing them, Aubrey had froze.

All of the E.R.'s staff vast skill and expertise proved inadequate. They couldn't save her parents' friends. Within the hour, Uncle Jesse and Aunt Maureen were both dead.

Aubrey lost more than two patients and more than two family friends that sad and terrible day. She lost a part of herself. And though she wouldn't admit it to anyone, she was terribly afraid she might never find it again.

"Hey, you okay?" Gage reached over and tucked a stray lock of hair behind her ear, a gesture so familiar, Aubrey's heart ached. He let his fingers linger. "You seemed lost for a second there."

He couldn't be any closer to the truth.

Something stirred inside her at the intimate contact, and it wasn't revulsion. Her eyes involuntarily sought his. Emotions, some old, some new, filled her. Without intending to, she let out a soft, "Oh."

A horn beeped, then another. The moment, or whatever it was, abruptly ended.

Gage grabbed his hat off the dash and swung around. "Traffic's moving. I'd better get back to my truck."

"I think that's a wise idea." Aubrey started the SUV with shaky fingers. She was never so glad to be surrounded by rude and impatient drivers.

"How about you and me pick this up later where we left off?" Without waiting for her answer, he stepped outside.

Another chorus of horns blared. Aubrey began to inch ahead, forcing Gage to slam the door shut. "How about we not?" she muttered under her breath.

In the next instant, he was on the run, his arm raised high in a parting wave.

Aubrey let out a frustrated grumble. Five minutes alone with him and look what happened. She let him touch her and stare at her…and…comfort her. Did she not possess so much as a smidgen of self-control?

GAGE PICKED UP his cell phone and punched in his friend's number.

"KSLN newsroom."

"Marty, it's me."

"Hey, buddy. What have you got?"

"Traffic's moving," Gage said. "Slow, but steady. I'll let you know more when I reach the accident scene."

"The tow truck just hit town. Should be in your vicinity within the next few minutes. My guess is only the northbound lane's open."

"Nothing coming at me, so I'd say you're right."

Gage kept Aubrey's silver SUV in sight. He planned on tailing her the entire way to Blue Ridge. The road was notoriously rough in places and in her present distracted state of mind, she might not be paying close attention.

"Did you hear the latest on the Denver fire?" Marty asked.

"Got the call a half hour ago. Thirty-five percent contained as of this afternoon. Assuming the weather holds, it'll be fifty percent by the morning."

"Kelli's already unpacked my bags. She was furious I might miss our six-month anniversary."

"Newlyweds. Every month is a reason to celebrate."

"That's fine with me." Marty chuckled. "Kelli really knows how to celebrate, if you catch my drift."

Gage did. All too vividly, in light of his recent encounter with Aubrey.

"You disappointed about the fire?" Marty asked.

"Not at all."

"Huh! I figured you'd be raring to go. It's been almost two weeks since the last one."

"Aubrey arrived today."

"Ah. That's right. The ex-wife is back in town. How'd it go?"

"Good and bad." Gage gunned the accelerator and passed a van. Only three vehicles now separated him and Aubrey's SUV. "Good because she let me get within ten feet of her without clamming up. Not that she talked a mile a minute."

"And bad because…?"

"She looks great." *And feels great, too.* Gage's fingers still tingled from when he'd brushed her hair back from her face.

"Gage," Marty said, his tone patient. "Need I remind you

the lady ran out on you without so much as a 'see ya around, it's been swell'?"

"She didn't run out on me. The divorce was a mutual decision."

"Thanks to her father's interference."

"Can't blame him for everything. If she'd really wanted to stay married to me, she wouldn't have left." *Or, I could have gone with her,* thought Gage. "But I see your point."

"You were a walking train wreck afterward. Are you sure you want to put yourself out there again?"

"No. But you should have seen her."

Gage recalled Aubrey hurrying across the gas station parking lot. Short denim skirt. Short little top. Short red hair. The only thing long about her had been her legs. He'd never seen so much of their tanned length exposed in public. The Aubrey he remembered lacked the confidence to show off her body. Gage had to admit he liked the change in her.

In fact, everything about her was different, including her green eyes. They were the same color, but their former vividness had been replaced by wariness and a sadness he didn't think had anything to do with him or their breakup.

He often wondered what might have become of them if her father hadn't shown up that night, waving a carrot in front of Aubrey's face. Her decision to return to college hurt Gage, but the passing years had given him an adult perspective he lacked at twenty. He understood, at least in part, some of her reasons and didn't disagree with them.

Blue Ridge offered little opportunity for anyone with an ambition outside of ranching. He of all people knew that. Aubrey dreamt of following in her father's footsteps her whole life. Bombing her first year at college took a little of the wind from her sails, but it hadn't thrown her off course.

No, Gage did that when he proposed marriage.

Marty made a disgruntled sound into the phone, distracting Gage.

"Be careful, buddy. A hot ex-wife back in town is no reason to go all stupid."

"Quit your worrying," Gage answered, returning his focus to Aubrey's SUV. "I'm not planning anything."

But he was. He'd seen the spark igniting in Aubrey's eyes when he'd touched her. And while he wasn't ready to go "all stupid" as Marty put it, he did want to explore possible options. Risky, yes, but the plain truth was, he'd never cared for a woman the way he had Aubrey. One look at her again and he wasn't sure he ever would.

The only way to discover for sure if Aubrey reciprocated any of his feelings was for him was to see her again.

Already his mind was formulating a plan. One that would ensure he and Aubrey crossed paths frequently during her stay in Blue Ridge.

Chapter Two

Aubrey flopped over onto her side, pulled the bedsheet up around her neck and cracked open one eye. A field of tiny pink tulips filled her vision, more faded than they'd been the last time she slept in this room, but still the same.

She and her sister chose the wallpaper, back when she was four and Annie three. It was the first summer they'd stayed in Blue Ridge. Grandma Rose had wanted the girls to feel at home, so she and Grandpa Glen drove them into Pineville for the day and let them pick out paint, wallpaper, bedspreads, matching sheets and a lamp at the home decorating store. Being little girls, they went with a pink color scheme.

Grandma Rose never changed a thing. Every summer for the next fourteen years, Aubrey and Annie spent their nights in twin beds, slumbering amongst pink tulips. Until the summer ten years ago when, fresh from a quickie Las Vegas wedding, Aubrey had moved out of her grandparents' house and into an old motor home parked behind the barn on the Raintree ranch.

Thinking of Gage reminded her of the two of them in her SUV yesterday. One little touch of his fingertips, one brush of her hair, and she'd gone soft and gooey inside. Old habits were definitely hard to break. Groaning, Aubrey drew the bedsheet over her head and buried her face in her pillow.

"Aubrey," her grandmother hollered from her bedroom across the hall.

"Coming!" Aubrey sprang out of bed, glancing at the alarm clock as she did. The red numerals glowed 8:16 a.m. *Yikes!* No wonder her grandmother was hollering. Throwing a robe on over her pajamas, she hurried through the door.

"Were you still sleeping?" Grandma Rose asked when Aubrey entered her room.

"I could have sworn I set the alarm before I went to bed."

"It's all right. You needed your sleep. I could tell when you arrived yesterday that you were tired from the drive."

More frazzled than tired, thought Aubrey. She'd seen Gage tailing her the entire way from Pineville to Blue Ridge and couldn't shake the feeling he was going to prove as difficult to outrun during her stay here as he was on the road yesterday afternoon.

"That's no reason for me oversleeping." Aubrey positioned the wheelchair by the side of the bed, then helped her grandmother to a sitting position. "Do you need to use the bathroom?"

"If you don't mind."

"That's why I'm here."

Over the next thirty minutes Aubrey saw to her grandmother's needs, getting her bathed and dressed and otherwise ready to face the day. When they were done, she wheeled her grandmother to the kitchen and got her situated comfortably at the table. It still shocked Aubrey to see how small and frail her grandmother had become. When she'd arrived yesterday and glimpsed the older woman napping in a recliner, only the presence of Mrs. Payne, the neighbor, had kept Aubrey from crying out in alarm.

"What do you feel like eating this morning?" Aubrey asked as she made a pot of coffee.

Like the bedroom she and her sister had shared, there were no significant changes in the kitchen's decor, either. Coffee was stored in the second largest of four ceramic windmill canisters on the counter. The others held flour, tea bags and sugar, in that order.

"Just toast. And maybe some of that calcium-enriched orange juice," her grandmother answered.

"Is that all?"

"I haven't recovered my appetite since the accident."

No wonder her grandmother had lost so much weight. Aubrey remembered the breakfasts served in this kitchen as being hearty enough to satisfy a crew of lumberjacks.

"Well, maybe we can fix that while I'm here." She placed two steaming mugs of coffee on the table, then opened a cupboard where she knew she'd find a loaf of bread.

"I'm so glad you came, dear." There was genuine pleasure in her grandmother's voice, along with a hint of sorrow. "I'll try not to be a burden."

Aubrey went over to her grandmother and placed an arm around her shoulders. "Don't talk like that. You're no burden whatsoever."

"I suspect your father didn't want you coming here. As far as son-in-laws go, he's everything a mother could ask for. But he can be a little dictating at times."

"A *little?*" Aubrey laughed and took the chair beside her grandmother.

Dictating did indeed describe Alexander Stuart. He was a man used to wielding authority. And though he meant well and loved his family dearly, he sometimes treated his wife and daughters like rookie interns who needed to be browbeaten into shape.

The first time Aubrey openly defied him had been the end of her freshman year at college. Unable to cope with the pressures and high expectations put on her, she'd escaped to Blue Ridge and married Gage.

It wasn't the last time she defied him, either. And while her father had backed off over the years, he still attempted to sway her when he felt she was making a wrong decision.

Like now.

Alexander Stuart had preferred to hire a caregiver for his mother-in-law so that Aubrey could remain in Tucson and face her career crisis head-on. He disapproved of her "running off and hiding in Blue Ridge again" as he'd called it. But Aubrey didn't tell her grandmother that.

"I'm so glad you're here." The older woman smiled warmly. "I've missed you."

Aubrey covered her grandmother's hand. "I've missed you, too."

Sitting there in the homey kitchen she remembered so well, Aubrey was glad she'd returned to Blue Ridge. She wanted nothing to tarnish or otherwise ruin her stay. So, for her grandmother's health and well-being and her own peace of mind, she'd learn to live—temporarily—in the same town with Gage.

She rose from the table, brimming with determination. "How about some eggs with that toast, Grandma?"

"Maybe one. Fried." The smile tugging at her grandmother's lips was conspiratorial. "I'm supposed to be watching my cholesterol."

"One fried egg coming up. And we won't tell your doctor I corrupted you." Aubrey fixed an egg for herself, as well.

The two of them enjoyed a leisurely meal that started with a discussion of Grandma Rose's care and diet and ended with an unexpected barrage of banging noises emanating from the front porch.

Aubrey put down her coffee mug and automatically stood. "What is that?"

"I have no idea." Grandma Rose peered through the doorway leading into the living room.

At the sound of the front door opening, Aubrey hastily retied her knee-length robe, which suddenly felt tissue-paper-thin, then plucked her tousled hair. "Somebody's here." She'd forgotten what it was like living in a small town. Friends and neighbors frequently stopped by without phoning first and doorbells were for strangers.

"Morning," Gage called from the living room. "Anybody home?"

Aubrey dropped back into her chair.

"We're in the kitchen," Grandma Rose called back, obviously delighted at the prospect of a visitor. "Have you had breakfast yet?"

Gage stopped in the doorway, smiling broadly. Rather than his cowboy hat, he wore a baseball cap, which he removed as he entered the room and bent down between the two women to plant a kiss on Grandma Rose's cheek. "Mom already fed me. But I'll take a cup of coffee if there's extra."

Grandma Rose tittered like a schoolgirl. "Why, of course there's extra."

He leaned toward Aubrey. She shied, momentarily alarmed he intended to kiss her cheek, too. But he just winked.

"Stay put," he said. "I'll get my own."

Aubrey had every intention of staying put. Silly, she supposed. Gage had seen her wearing far less than pajamas and a thin robe during their marriage. Heck, the outfit she wore yesterday exposed more bare skin than this one. Her fingers gravitated toward the hem of the robe. The movement must have caught his eye, for he looked down, and his smile widened.

Damn him.

Her first instinct was to lower her head. She resisted and met his gaze head-on.

Like the previous day, heat crept up her neck, all the way to the tips of her ears. Still she stared. "Clean mugs are in the cupboard to the right of the sink," she said.

"What brings you by this morning?" Grandma Rose asked. "And don't tell me it's the smell of brewing coffee."

She appeared oblivious to Aubrey's discomfort. The Raintrees had always been friendly with her grandparents. Fortunately, Aubrey's and Gage's impulsive and short-lived marriage hadn't affected that friendship. Given the two families' long-standing history together, Gage was probably a frequent visitor to her grandmother's house.

"I'm here to start work on the handicap renovations."

"What?" Aubrey and her grandmother said in unison.

"You did advertise for a handyman?" Gage peered at them

from over the brim of his mug, then took a sip of coffee. "I saw the notice posted on the bulletin board outside of Cutter's."

There were two markets, if one could call them markets, in Blue Ridge. Cutter's was the larger of the two, not much more than a convenience store with a modest produce bin, while the town's one and only gas pump could be found at the Stop and Go.

"I did," Grandma Rose exclaimed. "But surely you can't be answering the ad. When in the world would you have time, what with working at the ranch and all?"

Gage propped a hip on the edge of the counter in a casual stance that somehow managed to be sexy, too.

"Well, it's not just me. We're splitting the job between all of us in the volunteer fire department. I'm building the wheelchair ramp for the front porch. Gus will change out your round doorknobs for lever ones, and Mike's installing a grab bar in your bathtub. Anything else you need, Kenny Junior will handle."

"Gage is the captain." Grandma Rose beamed. "He was promoted after Bob Stintson and his wife moved to Show Low."

"Really?" So, Aubrey thought, he had stuck with firefighting. No surprise. Gage always had a sense of adventure. He was the one who suggested they elope, after all.

"You know we're raising money for some new equipment." Gage directed his statement at Grandma Rose. "We figured this would be a good chance to build the fund and help out a loyal contributor at the same time."

"Why, I'm…." She placed a hand at her throat. "I'm just thrilled. Thank you, Gage. Thank all the boys for me. Now you swear this won't be an inconvenience? I heard from Martha Payne yesterday your father has suffered another gout attack."

"He's not so bad. I think he'll be up and around in a couple of days. Hannah can handle things for one morning," Gage said, referring to his younger sister.

Aubrey thought she noticed a bit of tension in the lines around Gage's mouth. She remembered Mr. Raintree as being a somewhat hard and inflexible man, on par with her own father. She and Gage always shared that commonality. If Mr. Raintree was laid up, he probably depended on Gage and Hannah to run the ranch. The work was constant and difficult, she knew firsthand from her brief residence there.

"Are you sure?" her grandmother asked. "I don't want to be the cause of any...discord."

"Forget it." He dismissed her worries with a casual shrug. "I'd be here helping even if you hadn't advertised for a handyman."

Aubrey believed him. Gage adored her grandmother, and she him. But, as Aubrey watched their exchange, she couldn't help feeling something was amiss in the Raintree family.

"Dad's just being his usual grumpy self," Gage went on.

Her grandmother nodded in understanding. "Gout is no picnic."

"Probably less painful than a broken hip." He shifted his weight to his other foot, looking quite at home and in no hurry to start the renovations.

"It's been tough going so far," Grandma Rose said, smiling, "but I expect to improve rapidly now that my granddaughter is here. I couldn't ask for a better nurse."

Gage toasted Aubrey with his coffee. "Here's to granddaughters."

Bringing her mug to her lips, she drained the last bit of coffee. "Grandma, we should probably get a move on."

Her grandmother's appointment wasn't until early afternoon, but Aubrey wanted Gage out of the house. The three of them sitting around the kitchen having a friendly chat reminded her too much of days gone by.

"Where you headed?" he asked, not taking the hint and not moving an inch.

"Physical therapy," Grandma Rose told him.

"Sounds like fun."

"It's hard work," Aubrey corrected him.

"I don't doubt it." Unfazed by her brusque tone, Gage

polished off his coffee, rinsed out his mug and placed it in the dishwasher. "And speaking of hard work, I should get cracking."

Aubrey blew out a huge sigh when she heard the front door shut behind him. How long, she wondered, would it take to build the wheelchair ramp? More importantly, how long until she could comfortably share the same air space with him?

Getting Grandma Rose ready for their trip to Pineville didn't take long. She obviously wished to be self-sufficient eventually and would do whatever was required of her to achieve that status. Because morale played an important part in the recovery of someone in her grandmother's condition, Aubrey encouraged her.

Afterward, she helped her grandmother into the recliner so that she could watch her favorite soap opera. During the show, Aubrey showered and dressed. When she finished, they still had a good half hour to kill before they had to leave for the rehabilitation center in Pineville.

"Wheel me out onto the porch, dear," Grandma Rose said, using the remote to shut off the TV, "so I can see how Gage is doing with the ramp."

Aubrey tried to come up with a valid argument. "Are you sure? You have a big afternoon ahead of you and don't want to overdo it."

"I'd like to know how I can overdo it by just sitting."

"It's warm out there."

"Nonsense." Grandma Rose leaned forward and braced her hands on the armrests. "I can tolerate a little heat."

Aubrey reluctantly complied with the request, the wheelchair bumping as it rolled over the threshold and onto the porch. She thought about asking Gage if he could replace the threshold with a flatter one, then caught herself. Asking one of the other guys might be a better approach.

The first sight to greet her as she stepped outside was Gage's pickup truck parked in the driveway. The emblem on the door, she now noted, was some kind of flame with initials in the center. He'd lowered the tailgate and was using it as a makeshift workbench. The second sight to greet her was Gage. He stood with his back to them, bent over a circular saw and cutting wooden planks. She tried not to notice him, but her eyes kept darting across the yard to where he worked.

His shoulders were broader than she remembered, the muscles more defined and prominent. He might have grown another inch or two. Then again, maybe he just stood straighter and taller. Either way, maturity agreed with him. Were he another man, Aubrey might find the changes appealing.

When the plank Gage was cutting split neatly into two pieces, he shut off the saw and looked up. "Hey, there." Removing his ball cap, he ran fingers through sweat-dampened hair, then flung it onto the tailgate as he came toward them. "Need a hand?"

"No, I—"

"Good heavens, Gage," Grandma Rose interrupted. "You must be dying of thirst. Get him a glass of lemonade, will you, Aubrey?"

Setting the brake on the wheelchair, she gratefully retreated into the house. Maybe by the time she came back with his lemonade, he'd be working again.

No such luck.

He was sitting in the chair closest to Grandma Rose when Aubrey stepped outside.

"Thanks," he said, as he shot to his feet and reached for the plastic tumbler she carried.

She gave it to him and when he'd sat back down, she inched toward the door. "I have a few things to do around the house before we leave for Pineville."

"There's nothing that can't wait until later," Grandma Rose said, motioning with her hand. "Sit down and visit for a while."

Gage grabbed one of the other chairs and dragged it over next to his. Flashing his trademark sexy grin, he patted the seat. "You heard your grandmother. Sit and visit for a while."

To a casual observer, the invitation appeared innocuous enough. Aubrey knew better.

He drank half the lemonade in one long swallow. "Whew! That hit the spot." He then lifted the plastic tumbler to his forehead and rested it there. "Awfully hot for June."

"Do you remember the day you and Gage first met?" Grandma Rose didn't wait for a response and just prattled on. "It was at Sunday school. You were about four and Gage must have been, oh, five or six. You had on that pretty pink dress I liked with the big white sash. We had such a time with your hair, trying to make it look nice." She made a tsking noise. "A few weeks before arriving here, you and your sister decided to play beauty parlor. Annie, the little dickens, cut a huge chunk of hair out of the left side of your head. Your poor mother cried for days."

Aubrey had no desire whatsoever to walk down memory lane. Gage clearly didn't share her sentiment and enthusiastically participated in the discussion, bringing up one youthful indiscretion after the other.

Crossing and uncrossing her legs, Aubrey endured the small talk. Because of Gage, she'd lived exclusively for the summer when she and Annie would stay in Blue Ridge. For nine straight weeks, their parents visited various hospitals across the country where their father would demonstrate the latest medical advance he'd made in the field of cardiovascular surgery.

Their mother, Carol May Stuart, had been raised in Blue Ridge, having met their father at college. They both liked the idea of their daughters being exposed to the same grassroots upbringing she experienced. The girls loved Blue Ridge; their grandparents loved having them stay. It had been a perfect arrangement. Until the summer after Aubrey's freshman year at the University of Arizona when everything went to hell in a handbasket.

"Do you remember the day you came home and announced you'd eloped?" Grandma Rose's smile turned sentimental. "I was so happy for you both."

If Gage was ill at ease with her grandmother's reminiscences, he didn't show it. His attention didn't waver from

Aubrey once while the older woman recounted the incident. Not that Aubrey had made eye contact with him. But she could feel his stare just as surely as if he'd reached over and laid a hand on her.

"I remember everything," he said in a husky voice.

She remembered everything, too. And despite the scalding temperatures, a shiver ran through her.

Perhaps sensing Aubrey's discomfort, Grandma Rose slapped the arms of the wheelchair. "Would you look at the time." No one had so much as glanced at their watch. "We'd best be on the road, hadn't we, Aubrey?"

"Yes," she mumbled and gratefully rose.

Gage also stood and grabbed the back of her chair, pulling it out. She couldn't help herself and looked at him. Given the sexually charged atmosphere in the SUV yesterday, she fully expected desire or longing to be reflected in his features. What she saw there caught her off guard and affected her far greater.

Sadness and, unless she was mistaken, regret. For their marriage, she wondered, or that it ended? She couldn't tell, and maybe that was for the best.

"And I need to get back to work. That ramp won't build itself." Gage's smile vanquished all trace of negative emotion from his face. "Can I help you into the car, Rose?"

"Yes, thank you. That would be nice. Aubrey, fetch my purse for me, will you? It's on the kitchen counter."

"Sure, Grandma."

They were leaving at last. Retrieving her grandmother's purse first and then hers, Aubrey headed back outside just as Gage was assisting Grandma Rose into the SUV. The scene was tender enough to give Aubrey pause.

He had no sooner buckled her grandmother's seat belt when a series of loud beeps cut the air. Stepping away from the SUV, he reached for the radio hooked to his belt. Aubrey remembered seeing similar communication devices being used by the local ranchers. After listening to a garbled voice,

Gage depressed a button and returned the radio to his belt, a frown creasing his brow. "I have to leave."

"Problems at home?" Aubrey asked.

"No."

Without so much as a wave goodbye, he abandoned Grandma Rose and hopped into his truck. Throwing it into Reverse, he tore out the driveway, the tires spewing a shower of gravel and dirt. He hadn't even bothered to put the tailgate back up. His ball cap sailed out and landed at the end of the driveway.

"What the heck was that all about?" Aubrey asked after retrieving the cap and loading the wheelchair into the back of her SUV. It annoyed her that Gage would take off and leave the ramp half-done, not to mention a mess in the front yard.

"I suppose he got called to a fire," Grandma Rose answered.

"What fire?" She scanned the nearby rooftops. No telltale plume of gray-black smoke billowed skyward.

"In the mountains somewhere, I suppose." She peered out the window. "Or anywhere in the state. Once they went to California and twice to Colorado."

Aubrey jammed the key in the ignition, inexplicably irritated. "The volunteer fire department doesn't travel outside Blue Ridge."

"No. But the Blue Ridge Hotshots do. Gage is also a wilderness firefighter."

Aubrey's mind grappled with the unexpected information. "Since when?"

"For a while now. During the summers, mostly. He does something else with them the rest of the year, too, but I don't know what. Part-time, of course. He still works the ranch with the family."

"You're kidding."

"He didn't tell you?" Grandma Rose looked surprised.

Aubrey shook her head. "No one did."

Her family seldom talked about the Raintrees after the divorce. Aubrey's father resented Gage and flew off the handle every time his former son-in-law's name was

mentioned. Because his outbursts had accounted for any
number of unpleasant family gatherings, Aubrey opted to
keep the peace and stopped asking about Gage. News occasionally made it her way via her grandmother, but not with
any regularity.

She had yet to start the SUV, and the vehicle's interior temperature quickly escalated. Turning on the engine, she set the
air-conditioning on maximum before pulling out of the driveway.

The drive to Pineville took about an hour, not all of which
was filled with conversation. During the frequent lulls,
Aubrey's mind drifted to Gage. Besides being captain of the
Blue Ridge Volunteer Fire Department, he was also a wilderness firefighter. Amazing.

Mountain fires had been in the news too often during the
last few years for her not to know what a Hotshot was and
how important they were to the safety and preservation of
Arizona's endangered high country.

She'd always assumed—along with most people in Blue
Ridge—that Gage would follow in his father's footsteps and
take over management of the Raintree Ranch. To discover
he'd chosen a different profession, one as dangerous and
challenging as a wilderness firefighter, intrigued her.

And being intrigued by Gage was a complication she
neither wanted nor needed in her life right now.

Chapter Three

THE SMELL OF chicken enchiladas, homemade pizza and hot apple pie commingled, filling Aubrey's SUV as she drove the main road through town the following morning. From their resting place on the floor in front of the passenger seat, the foil-wrapped food dishes rattled and shook in protest with every bump, pothole and sharp turn.

Buildings and landmarks marked Aubrey's short trip, most familiar, a few new. The feed store, the one-room public library and Mountain View Realty's log cabin-style office building were the same as she remembered. A life-size wooden statue of a bear now stood in front of the Blue Ridge Inn, its big paw raised in greeting.

How, Aubrey asked herself, had she let her grandmother coerce her into running this errand? Some of the Hotshot crews, as reported by her grandmother's neighbor, Mrs. Payne, had taken over the Blue Ridge community center. "A satellite fire camp of sorts," she'd said, and explained a little about how the twenty-member crews rotated shifts. In a show of support, many of the townsfolk prepared food for the wilderness firefighters, who used the community center to eat, sleep and otherwise relax before returning to action.

According to recent reports, the blaze had been raging in the mountains twenty-five miles east of Blue Ridge since yesterday, apparently started from the smoldering remains of an illegal campfire left by recreationists. It didn't take much to ignite a fire during the hot, dry Arizona summers.

Originally, Mrs. Payne had planned on delivering the food items. But the two older women got to chitchatting and decided Aubrey should do it. That way, they could work on a baby quilt for Mrs. Payne's newest grandchild. Aubrey agreed, only because she didn't have the heart to deny her grandmother the opportunity to spend an enjoyable hour with a friend. And it was for a good cause.

Besides, what were the chances of Aubrey running into Gage anyway?

That's what you said at the gas station, a small voice inside her teased.

"Shut up," she told the voice as she pulled into the community center parking lot.

Aubrey had spent every spare minute not dedicated to her grandmother's care thinking about Gage and his second job. She remained glued to the radio and TV news for updates on the fire. She'd even gone so far as to research Hotshots on the Internet, using the laptop computer she'd brought with her.

Holding the box of food dishes to her chest, she used her shoulder to push open the heavy door leading into the community center. From the number of vehicles in the parking lot, she expected quite a few people to be inside. The actual count was considerably more.

A dozen or so cots took up one corner of the huge, airy room, many of them occupied. Metal chairs surrounded a TV, which sat on the small, homemade stage. Several stations had been created by arranging long tables into Us or Ts, their various purposes indicated by a cardboard sign taped to a corner.

"Hi, there. You bring a food donation?" The woman greeting Aubrey was about her age and looked vaguely familiar. Before she could place the face, the woman said, "You're Aubrey Stuart, aren't you? I heard you were back in town."

"That's me," Aubrey said, wishing she could remember the woman.

"You don't recognize me, do you?"

She smiled apologetically and shook her head.

"It's been a long time." The woman returned her smile. "I was Eleanor Carpenter. I'm Eleanor Meeks now. I used to live about a half mile up the road from your grandparents. You played sometimes with my younger sister, Beth. When you weren't playing with Gage, that is." Eleanor's eyes remained warm and friendly, but her smile turned impish.

"Of course." Aubrey was surprised by the delight she felt at running into a former acquaintance. "Nice to see you again." She shifted the box of food to her hip. "Are you volunteering here?"

"Yep. When I can arrange for someone to watch the kids, that is." She took Aubrey by the elbow and led her toward the kitchen located in the rear of the huge room. "Let's find a place for this food and then we can talk."

"Is your husband a Hotshot?" Aubrey asked.

"Was." Eleanor's smile faded. "He was killed two years ago in a burnover incident when the wind suddenly changed direction."

"Oh, my gosh! I'm so sorry." Aubrey instantly flashed on her parents' late friends, Jesse and Maureen. "I didn't—"

"It's all right." Eleanor reached into the cardboard box and removed one of the covered dishes. She placed it in an empty spot on the counter. "I won't lie and say things are always easy. But me and the kids, we're doing okay. Volunteering with the Hotshots helps." A shadow of grief crossed her face. It lasted only a moment and then she was smiling again.

Aubrey couldn't help thinking of Gage. Was he all right? Was he in danger? How long until he returned?

Some of the Internet Web sites she'd visited the previous night portrayed wilderness firefighting as a glamorous and exciting profession, the men and women as heroes. They were, but as an E.R. nurse, Aubrey knew better than most the not so glamorous and exciting side of firefighting.

"Hey, Eleanor," someone called. "Can you give us a hand? This idiot fax machine won't print."

"I'm the local Jane-of-all-trades." Eleanor sighed wearily, though she acted more pleased than put out. "Hang around, why don't you? If you're not in a hurry." She started off, then stopped and turned. "It's good to see you again, Aubrey. Welcome home."

Welcome home.

The phrase echoed in Aubrey's head. Though she had lived most of her life in Tucson, Blue Ridge had been home to her, too. Certainly the home of her heart.

"Thanks," she told Eleanor. "I think I will hang around."

Whatever malfunction had struck the fax machine, it perplexed not only Eleanor, but several others. While the group of workers stood over the machine—reminding Aubrey of surgeons and nurses in an operating room—she finished unloading the food dishes and went wandering the community center.

As she neared the front door, it flew open. A large group of Hotshots entered, dressed in dark brown pants, black T-shirts and heavy work boots with thick rubber soles. They were covered in grime, and the smell of smoke clung to them, nearly overpowering Aubrey.

She couldn't avoid hearing their conversation as they passed.

"I'm going to grab a quick bite to eat," said one of the tallest of the group. "What about the rest of you?"

Most concurred.

"I'm gonna hit the sack for a while." The speaker yawned noisily. "I haven't slept in two days."

The taller man slapped his buddy companionably on the back. "Take care of that arm first."

"This?" He held out the affected limb, and Aubrey noticed an ugly gash running the length of his forearm. "It's just a scratch."

"I don't care if it's a pinprick," the taller man said. "Take care of it."

"Yes, sir." The injured man veered away from the others and went behind a U-shaped station, where he dropped down into a metal chair and rolled up his sleeve. The cardboard sign taped to the table read First Aid.

Without stopping to think, Aubrey went over to him. "Can I help you with that? I'm a nurse."

He peered up at her, and his face brightened. "Sure."

She came around the tables and conducted a quick inventory of the available medical supplies. Then she took the man's arm and examined the cut. It was long and inflamed, but not deep.

"How did this happen?"

"A tree branch attacked me." His smile widened and took on a new appearance—that of a man interested in a woman. "You got to watch out for those fellows. They're sneaky. Catch you when you're not looking."

She released his arm, giving him the kind and helpful smile she reserved for patients. "I'm going to the kitchen for some water to wash this. I'll be right back."

"And I'll be right here."

In the kitchen, she found a small basin that she promptly filled with warm water from the faucet. She also found a stash of industrial paper towels and grabbed a handful. Not the best for cleansing wounds, but they'd do in a pinch.

True to his word, the man was waiting for her when she returned.

"You're back." He didn't mask his delight at seeing her.

Aubrey set the basin and paper towels down on the table near him and donned a pair of latex gloves. While she treated his wound, he engaged her in lively conversation. He was a good-looking man, despite the dirt and grime. And he didn't come on so strong that he offended her with his mild flirting. Another woman would probably flirt right back. But not her.

Aubrey met, and subsequently dated, any number of

available, attractive men. With every one, she waited for that telltale flutter of awareness in her middle. It rarely came, and the relationships tended to fizzle out, some sooner than others. Yet one glimpse of Gage bent over a circular saw cutting planks and she'd had enough flutters to lift her three feet off the ground.

"Are you a volunteer medic?" The injured man's question jarred Aubrey from her musings.

"No. I really just came by today to drop off some food donations." Aubrey had finished cleansing the wound and was applying an antibiotic ointment to the affected area.

"You live here?"

"Uh…yes and no." She opted for the condensed version, not wanting to go into her life story. "I'm staying with my grandmother for an extended visit. She's recovering from a broken hip. How about you?"

He shook his head. "Sacramento. Born and raised."

"And you belong to the Blue Ridge Hotshots?"

"No way," he scoffed and pointed with his free hand to the emblem on his T-shirt. It bore a resemblance to the one on Gage's truck. "I'm with the Sierra Nevada Hotshots."

"Really? I didn't know there were other firefighters here."

"There are four crews working the fire right now. Us, Blue Ridge, Albuquerque and the Tucson Hot Shots. More are scheduled to arrive tonight if the fire continues to spread."

"I just learned yesterday that Hotshots traveled to different states."

"We go wherever we're needed. Kind of like the marines." A dimple appeared in his cheek when he gave her a crooked grin. "So, are you free for dinner when this fire's done making the morning headlines, or do you have a boyfriend?"

"I…ah…." Why was she even hesitating? She absolutely did not have a boyfriend, and this seemingly nice, definitely handsome man had just asked her out. She tried to make her lips form the word no. "N-not really."

"Uh, oh. Too slow." The man—whose name Aubrey didn't

even know—chuckled good-naturedly. "And the eyes were a dead giveaway, too. Is he with the Blue Ridge Hotshots?"

"I don't have a boyfriend," she said, strong and firm with no hesitation this time.

"A wannabe boyfriend? Are you one of those Hotshot groupies?"

"Absolutely not!" She huffed indignantly. "May I remind you I'm holding your injured arm in my hands, and I'm not above inflicting pain."

His chuckle developed into a full-blown belly laugh. "As much as I'd be tempted to in this case, I don't steal another man's girl. But if you ever get tired of him, or he doesn't treat you right, give me a call. Sacramento's not so far away I can't find my way back here."

"Honestly, there's no one—"

"MacPherson! You're not giving this young lady a hard time, are you?" The taller man from earlier appeared, his jaw set in a no-nonsense frown.

"Who, me?" MacPherson pretended to be insulted.

"You'll have to excuse him, ma'am. He has a tendency to run off at the mouth. You have my permission to boot him where it counts if necessary."

"It's all right," Aubrey answered.

"Hey, Captain." MacPherson held up the arm that Aubrey had finished dressing. "She's a nurse."

"Are you?" the captain asked.

"Yes, I am."

"Are you a volunteer here?"

"Her boyfriend's one of the local crew," MacPherson interjected before Aubrey could answer.

"He's not my boyfriend," she protested, but no one paid her any heed.

The captain had made an attempt to wash up. His face and hands were scrubbed clean, if not the rest of him. "Have you ever considered volunteering? I'd be happy to introduce you to Marty Paxton, the Blue Ridge commander."

"Thanks, but no."

"Wilderness firefighting teams can always use skilled medical personnel."

Aubrey glanced around the community center, seeking a diversion. Where had Eleanor gone off to? "I can't. I'm the sole caregiver for my invalid grandmother." That sounded better than the truth.

Jesse and Maureen's deaths had done a real number on Aubrey, shaking her confidence to the core. No matter how hard she tried not to, she saw their faces in every trauma patient she treated. Aubrey believed she owed her patients the best possible care. How could she explain to the captain that she feared she might freeze the first time a seriously injured firefighter was brought in?

Thankfully, he took no for an answer. "Well, if you ever change your mind, I'm sure there'll be an opening for you."

"And you could always come to Sacramento if you get tired of this place." MacPherson bounced to his feet and shot her a look loaded with innuendo. "Thanks for the bandage job. See ya around, I hope."

"Nice meeting you, ma'am." The captain nodded curtly. "Let's go, MacPherson. We got a call while you were under the knife. Playtime is over."

"But we just got here."

The rest of MacPherson's complaint went unheard as the two men were joined by the remaining members of their crew. Moving as one, they rushed out the door. If they'd been riding horses, Aubrey would have expected to see a cloud of dust billowing behind them.

"You done?"

She turned at the voice and, seeing Eleanor, smiled. "There you are. I missed you earlier."

"Sorry about that. I got suckered into making a bunch of copies at the real estate office next door where I work. The owner is good about letting the Hotshots use his equipment."

"That's nice." It seemed to Aubrey the locals were more

than willing to assist the firefighters however they could. She'd forgotten how much she liked the we're-in-this-together attitude prevalent in small towns.

"Someone just brewed a fresh pot of coffee. Can I interest you in a cup?" Eleanor asked. "Or an iced tea? I'm scheduled for my break. We could catch up on old times."

If the promise of a caffeine pick-me-up wasn't enough, the hope shining in Eleanor's face would have persuaded Aubrey. "Sounds great." She reached into her jeans pocket for her cell phone. "Let me check in at home quick. Make sure everything's okay with my grandmother."

Home. There was that word again. She should probably be careful how she used it before someone—herself included—got the wrong impression. Look at the conclusion MacPherson had drawn thanks to one little slip of the tongue.

Why would anyone think she had a boyfriend?

"Have you seen Gage yet?" Eleanor asked after she and Aubrey found a quiet spot in which to curl up with their iced teas.

"Yesterday," Aubrey answered with forced nonchalance. "He and the other volunteer firefighters are doing the handicap renovations on my grandmother's house."

"Mmm. I think I heard that. Funny how neither one of you ever remarried."

Aubrey didn't rise to the bait Eleanor dangled. "Not really. I've been focused on my career for the past several years. Serious relationships have been low on my list of priorities." Not exactly the truth, but not a lie, either.

"I can certainly understand."

"What about your sister, Beth? Has she gotten married?" Aubrey's attempt to change the subject backfired.

"Last spring. To an insurance salesman in Show Low. You know, after you and Gage…after you left town, she made quite a play for him. He turned her down flat, which she took pretty hard. Of course, we all told her she was wasting her time. He was never interested in anyone but you. Oh, he's dated some. I mean, no man is made of stone. There was one gal in Pineville he hooked up with for a while. A technician for the phone company, I think." Eleanor smiled coyly. "But like you, serious relationships have been low on his list of priorities."

As it had yesterday on the porch with Gage and her grandmother, reminiscing made Aubrey fidgety. "Tell me about your children," she said. "Do you have any pictures?"

Trust a mother's pride in her offspring. To Aubrey's vast relief, Eleanor immediately switched gears and for the next several minutes they enjoyed an amiable conversation. One that didn't twist Aubrey's stomach into knots.

"I've really enjoyed visiting, but I need to get back to work," Eleanor said with reluctance. "I'm on duty until seven."

"It's been great. I hope we can do it again while I'm here."

"Oh." Eleanor's eyebrows lifted. "You aren't staying for good?"

"No. Only until my grandmother recovers."

If she did recover. The chances of an elderly person leading a fully independent life after breaking a hip weren't good. But Aubrey refused to dwell on statistics. Rather, she and her grandmother would take it one step at a time.

After a goodbye hug, Aubrey and Eleanor parted company. The TV blared in the background as Aubrey headed down the center of the large room. Men still slept in the cots, some of them snoring soundly.

She was about ten feet from the front door when it swung open and another group of Hotshots entered. These firefighters were wearing navy blue T-shirts, as opposed to black, she noted, and included a woman among their ranks. Knowing they must be tired and hungry, Aubrey stepped aside to let them pass, smiling at their nods and hellos, until the last man stepped through the door.

Upon seeing him, her smile froze.

Like the other Hotshots, he was dirty and grimy and smelled of smoke. Black smears covered his face and arms. Sweat plastered his short black hair to his head. A combination of sun, heat and wind had turned his tanned complexion dark and ruddy. Bits of debris clung to his clothing, and there was a jagged tear in the knee of his pants.

He looked tough and rugged and strong enough to hammer nails with his bare knuckles. He also looked sexy as hell.

The fluttering thing started again in Aubrey's middle. Only today it resembled propellers on a twin-engine plane rather than butterfly wings.

"Aubrey! What are you doing here?"

"Hi. I…uh…brought some food."

As a boy, he'd been cute. As a teenager, handsome. But Gage Raintree as a man fully grown was utterly breathtaking.

"Are you leaving already?" he asked.

"Actually, I've been here a while. And yes, I am leaving."

The other Hotshots had moved on ahead, leaving the two of them as alone as they could be in a large room full of people.

Gage took a step back and pushed open the door with one hand, the corded muscles of his arm standing out. "Here. I'll walk you to your car."

Oh, no, thought Aubrey. What now? Nowhere to run, nowhere to hide. The problem was, after getting one look at him, she really didn't want to do either of those things.

GAGE ENTERTAINED no doubts he would somehow get Aubrey alone and harbored no qualms about doing whatever was necessary to accomplish that end. He didn't blame her for her obvious reluctance; they had a lot of unresolved stuff still hanging over their heads. And just because he was ready and willing to tackle some of that unresolved stuff didn't mean she felt the same.

A sense of satisfaction filled him when she finally relented and agreed to let him accompany her outside. As a result, he now had the enjoyment of following her to her SUV. And it was definitely enjoyable.

She wore jeans today. Low-riders. And a snug little blouse

that revealed a modest band of creamy flesh. When she moved just right, he could see her belly button. A definite plus. Her short, bouncy hair had been pulled off her face with a headband, but several tendrils escaped, falling into her eyes.

Eyes that watched his every move.

Since running into Aubrey, Gage had dwelled on little else except her. Even the fire had taken a mental backseat, which was unusual for him. He tended to throw himself into firefighting to the exclusion of everything else, which caused a significant number of rifts with his family. To say his father disapproved of Gage being a firefighter was the understatement of the century.

When he and Aubrey reached her SUV, she reached for the driver-side door handle. Anticipating just such a move, he blocked her with his body.

"Sorry about leaving everything a mess yesterday," he said, leaning against the door. "When I get called, I have to report immediately."

"It's no problem." She dug impatiently through her purse for her car keys. "I moved what I could into the garage, if that's all right."

"I'll call Hannah. Have her stop by and pick it up."

"Don't bother. It's not hurting anything."

"Thanks. That'll save me making a second trip between the ranch and the house."

"How's the fire? I saw on the news it's only five percent contained."

A question. Good. Maybe she wasn't as skittish as she appeared. "We had a lucky break today with the weather, which is encouraging. But you can never predict for sure when it comes to fires, so I'm not packing my gear just yet."

"I admit I was a little surprised to learn you're a wilderness firefighter. When did that happen?"

"About four years ago. My friend Marty recruited me. I told you about him. He's with the Pineville radio station. We met when the old Hunt Museum and General Store burned down, and he came out to do a live broadcast."

"I took it for granted you ran the ranch with your dad." She gave a little shrug. "Since that was, well, that was always…"

"My plan. Yeah, well, it's still my dad's plan."

"He doesn't like you being a firefighter?" Her eyebrows knitted, then lifted. "I think he'd be proud."

Gage expelled a long breath. "It's not that he doesn't like me being a firefighter, just not now. Between his gout attacks and Hannah commuting back and forth during the week to the agricultural college in Pineville, running the ranch falls mostly to me."

"And firefighting has a tendency to cut into your chores."

"In a big way. It's a forty-hour-a-week job during the season. Double that when we're at a fire."

"What do you do when you're not fighting fire?"

"Clear roads of hazards, burn control fires, training. It's never-ending."

"You've taken on quite a load," she observed.

"More so now that we're participating in the drought study."

"Drought study?"

"For the federal government. All the ranches in the area have lost a lot of grazing land because of the drought. We didn't think we were going to make it for a while, and wouldn't have without the extra income from the study." He didn't tell Aubrey how very close the Raintrees had come to losing the ranch that had been in their family for five generations.

"I thought you liked ranching."

"I do." He caught her gaze and held it. "But I love firefighting, and I'm going to keep doing it despite my dad's objections."

"Good for you, Gage."

"Do me a favor, will you? The next time my dad and I have an argument, repeat those same words to me."

He grinned, attempting to lighten the mood and fend off the resentment perpetually gnawing at him. His father bent over backward to support his younger sister's ambitions, which were in keeping with the Raintree tradition of cattle ranching, but not his son's.

She smiled back. "Is he really that tough on you?"

"Tougher."

"What about hiring help?"

"We can't afford it."

"I hope you can find a compromise. Firefighting is special. Not that ranching isn't," she quickly amended. "But you make a real difference in the world." Genuine admiration tinged her voice, and his chest swelled.

"Like being a nurse?"

"Firefighting is nothing like being a nurse. You put your life on the line for others. That takes courage and daring."

"It's just a job."

"It's not just a job." She tilted her head and stared him square in the face. "I have to say, Gage, you really impress me. Not that I wasn't—"

She didn't have a chance to finish because he hauled her into his arms, lifted her onto her toes and brought her mouth to within a tiny fraction of his.

Her green eyes went wide. "If you're thinking of kissing me, think again."

"Oh, I'm going to kiss you, all right."

Deciding this was exactly the opportunity he'd unconsciously been hoping for, he swung her around and pinned her against the SUV door. She didn't run screaming, which was all the encouragement he needed. He then made good on his threat and kissed her soundly.

For the second time that day, he felt the searing sting of flames licking his body. Only these flames were the product of his own desire.

She didn't respond initially, and he could sense her struggle to remain unaffected. Gage would have none of it. He didn't merely seek entrance into her mouth with his tongue, he demanded it. And once inside, he made it his personal mission to affect Aubrey as much as possible. She held out for another few seconds, then conceded with a soft moan.

Mindless of the warm summer sun beating down on them and the occasional passing car or pedestrian, he kissed her over and over. Venturing from her mouth, he tasted a delicate earlobe and the sweet curve of her neck where it joined her shoulder. She shuddered and sighed, and he took her mouth again.

"Enough," she gasped when he finally allowed her to catch her breath.

Because he was fast approaching the point of no return, he eased back a step.

Aubrey pressed her palms to her flushed cheeks. "We can't do this. It's crazy."

"I want to see you. I think it's pretty obvious there's still a lot of attraction on both sides."

She worried her bottom lip and shook her head. "Not a good idea."

"I disagree." Gage's heart rate had finally slowed to something his overcharged system could tolerate. "Have dinner with me later this week. We'll talk."

Her dubious expression spoke volumes. "You're right about one thing. There is still a lot of attraction on both sides. But I've only been back in town a few days, and it's not like we've remained close through the years."

"Okay, w—"

She cut him off with a raised hand. "I'm not ready…not going to start dating you again. It would be a mistake. For a lot of reasons."

"Aubrey…"

"I'm out of here in six weeks when my leave of absence is over. And I don't think either of us wants another miserable parting. One was more than enough."

Gage was struck by the sudden pain clouding Aubrey's eyes. Pain because she'd hurt him and regretted it? Or had he hurt her? Truthfully, he'd never stopped to consider the possibility that his refusal to accompany her to Tucson might have been viewed by Aubrey as a form of rejection. Well, maybe he should consider it and consider it hard.

"I really have to go."

"Aubrey—"

She grabbed the door handle of her SUV and got in. This time, he didn't stop her.

"Goodbye, Gage. And good luck with the fire." She shut the door.

He stayed, watching her pull out of the parking lot and re-playing the last five minutes in his head. Kissing her had been great. Unbelievable. He didn't regret it for one second. But it was clear he'd pressured Aubrey for more than she was prepared to give. And if he didn't want to scare her off, he'd have to take a less headstrong approach.

Fortunately, Gage counted patience as one of his strong suits, along with perseverance.

If he'd learned anything as a Hotshot, it was when to fight and when to back off.

And that backing off didn't signify quitting.

Chapter Four

Gage was dirty, hungry and more tired than he could remember being in a long time. He wanted a hot shower, food—any food would do—and fourteen hours of uninterrupted sleep. In that order.

Standing at the back door of the ranch house, he indulged himself in a good, long stretch. When he finished, he treated the family dog, Biscuit, to an ear-scratching and head-patting combo. The fire hadn't been the worst one Gage had fought by any means, but there had been a few hairy moments, thanks to Mother Nature and her unpredictable whims. In addition, they were shorthanded, forcing all the Hotshots to work double shifts. The one time he'd visited the community center and saw Aubrey was his only break in three full days. But what a break it had been.

Since then, he'd repeatedly relived those minutes they kissed, lingering in particular on the taste of her warm and giving mouth. Not to mention the exact moment she melted against him, abandoning all efforts to resist. He thought less about her sudden turnaround. It surprised him how she'd gone from searing hot one minute to icy cold the next, and he intended to focus the sum total of his mental energies on resolving whatever prompted it.

Tomorrow, when he actually had some mental energy in supply.

He guessed it to be somewhere between ten and ten-thirty in the morning, if his blurry vision could be trusted. Good. His father and sister would be out somewhere working the ranch and not in the house. He'd persuade his mother to fix him breakfast while he showered, assuming she was home and not at work, then sleep until supper. She'd cover for him, and he could avoid a confrontation with his father until he'd had a chance to refuel and reenergize.

Luck, unfortunately, wasn't on Gage's side.

He stepped into the bright, sunny kitchen of the Raintree home and nearly collided with his father, who had apparently been on his way out the door.

"Morning, Dad." Gage quickly recovered and blustered through a friendly greeting. "How's the ankle?" He side-stepped the older man, making straight for the refrigerator.

Having raised two children, one headstrong and the other a handful, Joseph Raintree long ago perfected a stare worthy of freezing a guilty twelve-year-old in his tracks. Gage wasn't a kid anymore, but the stare still had the ability to immobilize him. He came to a grinding halt.

"You've been gone since Tuesday," Joseph said in a low voice. His lips hardly moved, yet each word struck Gage like a tiny bullet.

There wasn't more than a half-inch difference in their heights or the widths of their shoulders. And before the gout had gotten so bad, his father regularly gave Gage a run for his money in arm-wrestling matches. Steel-gray hair and a pronounced limp were the only visible signs Joseph had aged in the last twenty years. Inside the man, Gage knew, was a different story. Chronic pain had taken a toll on his father, in more ways than one.

"No message. No phone call. Your poor mother was worried sick."

"Wait just a minute." Gage exhaled and steadied himself. "I called home the minute I hung up from dispatch and talked to Hannah."

"Who didn't tell us until that evening where you were."

And this was somehow Gage's fault? "Her lack of communication skills isn't my problem."

"You're part of this family, which makes it your problem."

"Dad, even if she never said a word, you knew where I was." Gage bent over the sink, ran the cold water and splashed a handful on his face. "All you had to do was listen to the local news or pick up the phone and talk to a neighbor," he said after toweling dry. "Maybe leave this damn ranch once in a while and go into town."

"You will not take that tone with me."

"Dad—"

"What you *will* do is get dressed and finish the chores that need doing around here. Between you being gone and my gout, we're behind. The herd hasn't been moved to the south range yet, and we're almost a week late in filing the latest grazing study report."

"Didn't Hannah do anything while I was gone?" Anger and resentment built inside Gage, fed in large part by his utter exhaustion. His younger sister, it seemed to him, got away with as little work as possible. He didn't understand it, given her intention of taking over management of the ranch one day from their father. "I'm not the only one in this family capable of filling out forms." He looked past his father into the family room. "Where is Hannah, anyway?"

"Registering for summer school."

Gage slumped against the refrigerator and scrubbed his bristled jaw. "Summer school. How could I forget?"

How could he?

Hannah majored in agricultural management at Pineville College. She made the two-hour round-trip drive three days a week, arriving home too late to get much work done on the ranch. If not for a scholarship, she wouldn't be attending college at all.

Gage didn't begrudge his sister an education. Since he had no plans to follow in their father's footsteps, he was all for

Hannah doing it. And he himself had attended firefighting academy. But he did begrudge her their father's blatant favoritism. Hannah was separated from Gage by eight years and three miscarriages. As the long-awaited and much-wanted second child, she could do no wrong in the eyes of her doting parents.

"I thought we agreed Hannah was going to stay home this summer." Convinced his argument fell on deaf ears, Gage nonetheless persisted. "You know June and July are the busiest months of year for me."

"Can't be helped. She needs some class for next semester."

Gage pushed off the refrigerator. One class might be doable, if they all worked together.

"You'll have to pick up the slack," Joseph continued. "No more taking off for hours or days on end whenever the mood strikes you."

"I'm a Hotshot, Dad. Our job is to fight fires and save the very land your cattle graze on. What's left of it after four years of drought." A part of Gage's brain recognized the futility of his words, but the other part wouldn't shut up. "I also head the Blue Ridge Volunteer Fire Department. If this house were to go up in flames, I'd be the one driving the engine here. But I suppose even then you'd accuse me of taking off when the mood struck."

"You're twisting the situation around to suit your own purposes!"

"If I am twisting the situation around, I'm not the only one," Gage replied.

He broke eye contact first, ending their staring match, and tugged his filthy T-shirt free from the waistband of his pants. "I'm tired, Dad. I've had at most ten hours sleep in the past three days. Let me shower and take a nap. I'll fill out the reports and fax them in before supper. If sending them in sooner is that critical, Hannah can do it when she gets back."

Gage was well aware his sharp tone made him sound more like a frustrated teenager than an adult, but he was too tired to care. Both men turned when the back door flew open, and

Hannah burst into the kitchen, her long black hair caught up in a bouncy ponytail.

"Hey, big brother." The smile she showered on Gage lit up the room. If she ever put that smile to serious use, half the male population of Pineville College would be throwing themselves at her feet. "The prodigal son returns." Her glance traveled from Gage to their father, causing her smile to droop slightly. "Did I walk in on the middle of something? Oh, I get it," she said when no one answered. "None of my business."

"Actually, it is—"

Joseph didn't let Gage finish. He limped over to Hannah and bent down so she could plant a kiss on his cheek. "Did you get registered for your class?"

A stab of resentment penetrated Gage's empty and growling stomach.

"Two classes." Hannah extracted a paper from the back pocket of her jeans and waved it. "Remember?"

"Two?" Gage said, "I thought you were taking only one class."

"Agricultural accounting and animal industry 101. I start next week, Monday through Thursday. Sorry, Gage." The dark eyes she turned on him were the mirror image of his own in shape, size and color. Hers, however, were dancing and not the least bit apologetic despite her words. "These are accelerated classes, three hours each. I won't be home until afternoon. Hope that's not too much of a problem. Dad said you wouldn't mind covering for me."

"Funny, he didn't tell me that."

Joseph Raintree countered Gage's sarcasm with some of his own. "You weren't here to tell."

Gage made an abrupt dive for the door. He felt like if he stayed in the house a minute longer, he'd suffocate. "I'll do my best, but no promises. If I get called to a fire, I'm out of here. And speaking of getting out of here…"

"Where to you think you're going?" Joseph called after him.

"Somewhere quieter."

Gage no sooner shut the back door than it flew open and Hannah appeared.

"Wait. A letter came for you yesterday from the Forest Service. You might want it."

Gage took the letter from her outstretched hand and glanced at the return address. Could it be? So many weeks had passed, he'd long since lost hope. Tearing open the envelope, he prepared himself for bad news.

His luck, however, had taken a turn for the better.

Pleasure spread through him as he read the first paragraph. "I made it." The lowness of his voice took him aback, considering he wanted to shout his good news.

"Made what?"

Hannah stood at his elbow, trying none too discreetly to read the letter over his shoulder. Biscuit also stood nearby, tongue lolling and tail wagging, though his interest clearly lay in another petting.

"The list of candidates being considered for promotion. To crew leader." Gage surrendered to the grin tugging at his mouth. "I report Monday morning for my initial interview."

"Congratulations, big brother! That's awesome." She grabbed his arm and gave it an enthusiastic shake. "You so deserve this promotion."

"It'll mean more hours for me if I get it."

Hannah's expression said she couldn't believe he was worried about such an insignificant thing. "We'll manage."

"Thanks." Without thinking, he reached up and yanked affectionately on her ponytail.

Suddenly, his hand went still. How often had he done this exact thing in the years they were growing up? Too many times to count.

His resentment for his younger sister instantly faded.

"The monthly grazing reports are late. Think you can fax them out this afternoon, Hannah?"

"No problem."

"Call me on my cell phone if you have any trouble with them." He replaced the letter in the envelope and stuffed it in the front pocket of his T-shirt.

"I can handle the reports."

Gage nodded. "You've got what it takes to run this place, you know." And she did, if she ever quit fooling around and really applied herself.

His compliment brought a smile to her face. Gage was again struck by her prettiness.

"You sure you won't stay?" she asked. "Dad'll cool off in a couple of hours. He just likes to, you know, parade his authority."

"Parade his authority? That's a pretty big mouthful for an agricultural major."

"You'd be surprised at all the stuff I've learned in animal psych class that applies to people."

Gage chuckled. "See ya later, squirt. Tell Mom I'm sorry I missed her."

Ten minutes later he reached the end of the dirt road leading from the Raintree ranch to town. The pickup truck bumped as the tires hit pavement, tossing the various loose items that littered the front seat into the air. Gage headed east. He'd known his destination all along. It was the same place he always went to whenever he craved solitude.

Next to the community center sat a small block building that housed the volunteer fire department's sole engine. It wasn't the ragtag couch in the back room that drew Gage, but rather the small, run-down motor home parked behind the station.

The same motor home he and Aubrey had occupied during their brief marriage—only then it had been parked on the Raintree ranch.

Gage had continued to live in the motor home for several months after she left, foolishly hoping she might one day return. Even after he moved back into the ranch house and his old bedroom, he occasionally escaped to the motor home for some peace and quiet. A couple years ago, Joseph Raintree decided to dispose of the eyesore. Gage hooked the motor home to his pickup truck and hauled it to the fire station rather than the landfill, claiming it was for the guys to use.

So far, he was the only guy to use it.

The mattress in the motor home's sole bunk was lumpy and sagging, a condition fresh sheets and new pillows didn't improve. At the moment, however, it appealed to Gage more than the finest quality feather bed. And yet, when the driveway leading to the fire station appeared, he drove right past it and instead took the turnoff farther up the road, the one leading to Aubrey's grandmother's house.

He told himself he was just checking on the handicap renovations—to see what progress the others had made, if any, during his three-day absence.

It was a bald-faced lie, of course, and he darn well knew it.

AT THE SOUND of a vehicle door slamming, Aubrey placed the can of tuna fish she'd just opened on the kitchen counter and went into the living room. One of the volunteer firefighters must have stopped by to make another repair. Probably Kenny Junior. When he left the previous day, he promised to return and replace the front door threshold with a lower one.

His timing was actually good. Aubrey and her grandmother had recently finished a strenuous, yet productive, round of physical therapy. Bound and determined to walk on her own again, Grandma Rose had pushed herself hard. But rather than take a quick nap before lunch, as was her habit, she'd asked Aubrey to wheel her next door to Mrs. Payne's. The two friends were engaged in a heated race to finish the baby quilt before Mrs. Payne's grandchild made his grand entrance into the world.

Aubrey flung open the front door, ready to greet Kenny Junior, only it wasn't him. A different volunteer firefighter climbed the porch steps. This one younger, taller and…filthy from head to toe.

"Gage! What are you do—" She pushed open the screen

door and stepped out. Her hand stopped just short of taking his arm. "Jeez, are you all right? You look awful."

"Thanks." He moved as if each step resulted in excruciating pain.

"What happened? Were you injured?"

"Only a little." The crooked smile he aimed her way lacked its usual luster. "And not in the line of duty."

"Is that a joke?" By way of invitation, she opened the screen door and he followed her inside.

"Yes, it is. And evidently a bad one. You can blame my warped sense of humor on my dad. He didn't exactly give me a hero's welcome when I got home this morning."

"Oh, Gage." Because he obviously wanted to make light of an upsetting situation, Aubrey changed the subject. "I heard on the news this morning the fire is nearly contained."

"Pretty much done, except for the cleanup."

Once they were in the kitchen, Gage half sat, half tumbled into the nearest chair. He did look awful. She started to tell him he should be home in bed, then caught herself. Home, apparently, wasn't an option.

But that didn't explain why he was here, in her grandmother's kitchen.

"You hungry?" she asked instead of one of the dozen questions running through her head.

"I'd eat if you're offering."

"I am. And how about a shower?"

In response, a spark flickered in his tired eyes.

Her comment hadn't been the least suggestive, yet he'd taken it that way. Or was it she who'd subconsciously implied something suggestive?

"You can shower in the hall bathroom while I fix lunch," she added, just in case he'd misunderstood her. "I think there's still some of Grandpa's old clothes around here. They won't fit well, but they're clean."

He nodded, his smile tired, but grateful.

Some minutes later, she returned from rummaging through

an assortment of cardboard boxes stacked in the corner of the basement. The faded T-shirt would be too big around the waist and the men's cotton pajama bottoms too short in the leg for Gage, but it couldn't be helped.

She set the folded clothes on the floor outside the bathroom door. Her hand poised to knock, she instead waited, breathing slowly and listening to the sound of the running shower. Her heart beat a fraction faster. Gage stood on the other side of the door—stark naked and with hot water streaming down every inch of his body.

They'd showered together frequently during their marriage, the two of them squeezing into the motor home's tiny bathroom. She didn't recall lack of elbow room as being a problem. In fact, finding creative ways to utilize the cramped space had proven a thoroughly enjoyable experience.

Aubrey's vivid imagination went far afield before she roused herself and stifled it. Gage naked and showering wasn't something she needed to be thinking of, particularly after her little speech the other day about not being ready to date him again.

Besides, she doubted they could still fit in that tiny shower. She'd been skinnier then and so had Gage.

It might be interesting to try, the pesky voice inside her teased.

Yeah, interesting. And stupid.

Her leave of absence was up in five weeks, and she'd be returning to her job in Tucson, free, God willing, of whatever unreasonable fear had gotten a hold on her since Jesse and Maureen's deaths.

You hear me? she told the voice. *Stupid.*

The voice didn't answer.

Firming her resolve, Aubrey knocked briskly on the bathroom door and hollered, "The clothes are on the floor outside the door."

"Thanks," came a muffled reply, and then the water shut off. Oh…my.

Since continuing to stand there would only invite images of Gage drying himself, or drying her, Aubrey retreated to the kitchen, stopping first at the pantry for another can of tuna fish.

She made two sandwiches, slicing them diagonally before arranging them on a plate. Guessing Gage's appetite hadn't decreased in the intervening years since they'd dined together, she spooned out a bowl of cottage cheese and topped it with some of Mrs. Payne's home-canned peaches. Aubrey was just pouring a glass of milk when Gage came into the kitchen and promptly fell on the meal.

Conversation came to a complete standstill as he consumed the food with the speed and voracity of a grizzly bear newly awakened from a winter-long hibernation.

"Slow down," she warned, sitting in the chair beside him. "You'll choke if you're not careful."

He mumbled something that might have been, "Good," or "More." She wasn't sure which.

"Would you like another sandwich?"

Mouth crammed with peaches, Gage tilted his head from side to side.

"A half a sandwich?"

He nodded vigorously.

She took the liberty of pouring him a second glass of milk before rising and then took her sweet time fixing the half sandwich, all the while studying him discreetly from the corner of her eye.

Her late grandfather's clothes were indeed a poor fit, yet Gage managed to look sexy as hell in them. It might have been his still-damp, uncombed hair falling forward over his brow, or the bare feet and impressively muscular length of calf extending out from beneath the hems of the too-short pajama legs.

Yes, maturity definitely agreed with Gage Raintree. As did firefighting. No small miracle some woman hadn't snapped him up. In a town the size of Blue Ridge, he was surely one of the most eligible bachelors, if not *the* most eligible.

Having at last satisfied the need to gorge himself, he

slowed his rate of eating to something resembling that of a human being.

"Thanks. That hit the spot." He used the napkin she'd set out to wipe his mouth.

"When was the last time you ate?"

"Yesterday. Breakfast. Not counting the PowerBar I had for dinner last night."

"And before that?"

He arched one eyebrow. "Lunch the previous day. At the community center."

Ah. Where they'd kissed. Like Aubrey needed reminding.

Gage pushed his plate away, and she reached for his dirty dishes, thankful for the distraction.

"Leave them," he ordered in a low voice and placed his hand over hers.

"But—"

"The dishes can wait. Talk to me for a few minutes."

Aubrey watched, spellbound, as he folded her smaller hand into his larger one. "A-a-about what?"

His thumb traced small circles on the sensitive skin behind her knuckles and though she knew it was wrong as wrong could be, she let him continue.

"Why did you leave me?"

She tried to jerk her hand away, but he refused to relinquish it.

"Tell me," he said, holding her gaze as firmly as he held her hand.

Aubrey went still. "You know why. To return to school."

"Is that the only reason?"

"We were just kids, not ready for marriage. We couldn't even support ourselves without your parents' help."

"A lot of couples start out on a shoestring. They manage."

"Yes, if they're committed to each other they do."

"And you weren't committed to me?"

She chewed her bottom lip, debating on how to simplify a complicated answer. "High school was always easy for me.

I aced every class, sometimes without cracking a book. But college was a whole different story. You know that. I finished the second semester of my freshman year two-tenths of a grade point away from being expelled. My father didn't understand and came uncorked. I headed to Blue Ridge the day after school let out. To escape, though I told myself I was just taking a break. And then, there was you."

"Just like every summer," Gage said, his expression hard to read.

"No, you're wrong." She swallowed before continuing. Twice. "That summer we made love for the first time, and you proposed."

"You didn't have to accept my proposal if you really wanted to go back to school."

Aubrey stared out the kitchen window, seeing not her grandmother's yard but a view of the Raintree ranch from the motor home's back door.

"I didn't think I wanted to go back. I was in love in you." And she had been, body and soul. Probably from the first day they'd met in Sunday school.

"I'm glad to hear you say that."

She turned to look at him. "Tell me your proposal wasn't spontaneous and that you thought everything through before making it."

"It was spontaneous," he admitted. "But I don't regret it."

"Neither do I."

"We had six great weeks of marriage."

"One great week of marriage and five weeks of fighting," she corrected him.

He grinned. "That's not they way I remember it."

"Are you kidding?" She shot him a disbelieving look. "We fought more in those five weeks than most couples do in five years."

"We also made love more than most couples."

Yeah. At least ten of those times in a shower the size of coat closet.

"A great sex life isn't enough to base a marriage on."

He chuckled. "At least you admit the sex was great."

She smiled along with him as resisting was an exercise in futility. "That wasn't all we did right. We had a lot of fun, too, when we weren't at each other's throats."

"Not enough for you to stay married to me." His remark sobered them both. "Did you call your father and tell him to come get you?" His fingers tightened on hers.

"God, no! Is that what you thought?"

"It crossed my mind."

"I swear, Gage. His visit was entirely unexpected."

"So you hadn't planned on switching your major to nursing and not tell me?"

"That was strictly my father's idea." She sat up straight and squared her shoulders, steeling herself for the hard part. "But it was good one, and I'm grateful to him for having it. If I hadn't returned to Tucson and college, I might never have become a nurse."

Aubrey's father had appeared one night out of the blue, midway through the summer. He'd banged on their motor home door, insisting he speak with her. Once inside, he'd presented her with a proposition that included her changing her major from premed to nursing—a still difficult study course but with less pressure and less competition. He'd pulled some strings at the university and gotten her admitted into the nursing program. The catch was she had to return the third week of August in time for the fall semester.

Gage's grip on Aubrey's fingers relaxed. "I never wanted to hold you back. That wasn't the reason I proposed."

"You could have come with me to Tucson."

"And lived off your parents' charity? I don't think so," he scoffed.

Alexander Stuart had generously offered to supplement the newlyweds' income, enabling them to live in an apartment off campus while Aubrey attended school full-time. Gage's pride hadn't allowed him to accept the offer. She understood now what she hadn't then. It was important to Gage he be able to support himself and his wife without assistance. Not an easy task for a twenty-year-old with no college and no job skills besides ranching.

"We basically lived off *your* parents when you think about it," she ventured.

His eyebrows drew together. "That wasn't the same. We both worked on the ranch and earned our keep."

"You're right," Aubrey relented. She saw no reason to rehash a ten-year-old argument.

She didn't think her father had intended to break up her and Gage's marriage, not consciously anyway, but his attempt to facilitate her return to school had done exactly that by driving a wedge between her and Gage that grew wider with each day. Had they been older and more experienced, they might have found a solution. As it was, tensions mounted in the days following her father's visit, escalating in a final blowout that ended with Aubrey packing her bags.

"I couldn't win for losing," Gage said, letting go of her hand. "Not after your dad dropped his bomb."

"How so?" Her fingers felt oddly vulnerable without his wrapped around them.

"What choice did we have but to divorce? If I insisted you stay in Blue Ridge, you would have come to resent me for forcing you to give up your dream of working in medicine. Don't tell me you wouldn't have," he interrupted when she started to speak. "And if I went with you to Tucson and let your father support us, I'd have lost my self-respect and been miserable. Probably made both our lives miserable. The only other choice was a three-year separation, and I don't think our marriage could have survived while you finished college." He blew out a breath. "Whichever way I turned, I was screwed."

"Oh, Gage, I'm sorry." She hadn't realized until now how cornered and helpless he must have felt, and it saddened her.

He shrugged. "So, I admitted I was wrong. Then came the divorce."

"I wish I'd known that at the time."

"Would it have made a difference?"

"To be honest, I'm not sure. Maybe we were doomed from the beginning."

"Have you ever wondered what would've happened to us if we stuck it out?" he asked.

She considered lying. There was still a considerable attraction between them and she'd be courting trouble by giving him false hope. In the end, she opted for the truth. She owed him that much.

"Sometimes, sure. More so in the beginning."

Closing his eyes, he ran a hand through his nearly dry hair and down the back of his head. He looked so tired.

"You're ready to keel over," she said. "What say we call it a day, and you get some sleep?" Speaking for herself, Aubrey could use a break from all the emotional unloading.

"All right."

"Nap on the couch if you like. Grandma's next door at Mrs. Payne's. I'll take lunch over to them and stay awhile, leave you alone to get some rest."

"Nah." He stood, bracing one hand on the table and using the other to hold the sagging waistband of the pajama bottoms. "Think I'll head over to the volunteer fire station."

"You can't possibly work in your condition," she insisted in her best bossy nurse voice.

"Believe me, I'm going to sleep," he said with a laugh. "The old mot—" He stopped laughing and closed his mouth before continuing. "There's a bunk at the station where I can crash."

"Okay. In that case, you're free to go."

"Yes, ma'am."

He gave her a mock salute, and Aubrey shoved him through the kitchen door, laughing at the sight he made in her grandfather's pajama bottoms.

On the front porch, she waved goodbye as he backed his

pickup out the driveway, her emotions bouncing from one end of the spectrum to the other.

She was glad they'd talked and cleared the air of a few lingering issues. But by doing so, she opened herself to him, and the walls between them, walls she'd erected for both her own and his protection, had begun to crumble. If he kept holding her hand, kept staring into her eyes like he did, those walls might topple down completely.

Then where would she be? And more importantly, what would she do about it?

Chapter Five

Aubrey lightly pressed the back of her hand to her grandmother's forehead. The older woman lay in bed, her papery cheeks flushed a deep shade of pink and her eyes unusually bright.

"You mean to tell me, with all those years of training and all that fancy equipment, you still take someone's temperature by touch?"

"Why mess with success?" Aubrey didn't require a digital ear thermometer to tell her Grandma Rose's temperature was well over a hundred degrees and climbing.

"I'm fine. A bit of allergies is all." She pushed aside the sheet covering her as if to rise. "Happens every summer."

Aubrey snatched the edge of sheet and deftly replaced it. "Stay put."

"Like I have a choice," Grandma Rose groused. She'd made excellent progress during the past week with her physical therapy, graduating to short bouts around the house with a walker. But she was still a far cry from getting out of bed or a chair unassisted.

The past week had also been noteworthy for another reason. Aubrey hadn't seen or heard from Gage once since the day she'd made him lunch. Not that she had any reason to see or hear from him, she reminded herself firmly, nor did she necessarily *want* to. She would, however, like to know if everything was all right with him at home and if he'd resolved his differences with his father—strictly from the standpoint of a concerned friend, of course.

As promised, Kenny Junior had shown up to replace the threshold and Gus to change the round doorknobs to lever ones. She'd casually queried them both about Gage, but they hadn't seen or heard from him, either.

"How sore is your throat?" she asked her grandmother, banning thoughts of Gage to the back of her mind where they rightfully belonged.

"What makes you think I have a sore throat?"

Aubrey sighed. "You haven't touched the breakfast I brought you and made a terrible face when I forced you to take a few sips of apple juice."

"Are you always so mean to your patients?"

"Only when they try to pull the wool over my eyes. Now, how sore is your throat? Scratchy or agonizing?" She gently prodded her grandmother's neck beneath her jaw.

"Leaning more toward the scratchy side." Her grandmother winced and jerked away.

"Uh-huh."

"You don't believe me?"

"I believe you," Aubrey lied. She cradled her grandmother's face in her hands and turned her head toward the window.

"What are you doing?"

"Open your mouth."

Her grandmother obliged, but made it clear she didn't like Aubrey peering down her red and swollen throat.

Aubrey went into the small bathroom and returned a minute later brandishing a bottle of extra-strength acetaminophen. She leaned down and kissed her grandmother's burning forehead.

"I'll be right back. I'm going to the kitchen to break these up into smaller pieces for you."

There was no doubt in her mind Grandma Rose needed to see a physician. When she obediently popped the tablet pieces in her mouth and accepted the glass of water, Aubrey realized her grandmother was sicker than she let on.

"I'm taking you into Pineville, Grandma."

"What for?"

"To see your doctor. If he's not available, we'll go the hospital emergency room."

"Nonsense."

Aubrey went to her grandmother's closet and slid open the door. "Would you like to change first or go in your night-gown?"

"All this fuss over a little fever."

"You have a *high* fever."

"How would you know? You never even took my tempera-ture."

Aubrey rolled her eyes and returned to the bed with a floral dressing gown she'd found hanging on a peg just inside the door.

"In addition to a fever, your glands are swollen, and your throat looks like it's on fire. You're sick." She located her grandmother's slippers beneath the bed and pulled them out. "When people get sick, they visit the doctor."

"I hate going to the doctor." Grandma Rose stared into space, her chin set at a stubborn angle. "Ever since the accident, all I ever do is go to the doctor. I'm tired of it."

"I understand." Aubrey sat on the edge of the bed and took her grandmother's weathered hand in hers. "Getting old stinks. But it beats the hell out of the alternative." The blunt observation delivered with such candidness earned her a slight lowering of the chin from her difficult patient. "I love you, Grandma. And I don't want anything to happen to you. Certainly not anything I can prevent with a simple doctor visit."

The chin came down another inch.

"Now, quit being such a grump and let's get you dressed."

"All right," her grandmother said. "I'll go. But not to Pine-ville. Today's Thursday and the clinic is open."

"The clinic? I don't know…"

Blue Ridge lacked sufficient population to support a full-time physician and state-of-the-art medical facility. What the town did have was a two-to-three-day-a-week doctor and a one-room clinic built beside a ramshackle thrift store. The proceeds from the volunteer-staffed thrift store went to fund the clinic and the connecting helipad. In instances of serious illness or injury and when time was of the essence, patients were airlifted by helicopter to the hospital in Pineville.

Though she was well aware it had saved numerous lives, Aubrey didn't like thinking about the helicopter. Her grandfather had been airlifted out of Blue Ridge twice. And while reason told Aubrey neither the helicopter nor the clinic had anything whatsoever to do with her grandfather's death, she's still felt better taking her grandmother into Pineville.

"That Dr. Ferguson is a nice enough young man, I suppose. You haven't met him, he came here some years back after old Dr. Hunt retired," Grandma Rose babbled. "You remember Dr. Hunt, of course. He's the one who removed the fishhook from your scalp."

"How could I forget?" Aubrey slipped the dressing gown over her grandmother's head. "I still have the scar."

She'd been twelve and Gage thirteen. They'd hiked the two miles to Neglian Creek crossing alone, promising to return with enough trout for dinner. Gage took her hand in his the moment they'd left the main road and never let go. Midway through the afternoon, a misaimed cast on Aubrey's part resulted in disaster, made worse by their botched attempts to remove the hook. Gage, poor kid, had gone pale and shaky at the first drop of blood.

Aubrey had sympathized, given him a quick peck on the cheek and told him she'd be fine. He'd surprised them both when he took her by the shoulders and pressed his lips to hers. It had been their fist kiss. More followed each summer thereafter, increasing in frequency and intensity.

They'd discovered their secret spot earlier that same day. Tucked into the steep bank on one side of the creek and completely sheltered by the overhanging branches of a willow tree, it provided the perfect hideaway. For years afterward, they'd escaped there whenever opportunity presented itself.

It was the place they'd made love for the first time and, minutes later, where Gage had proposed.

"Dr. Ferguson is competent, mind you." Grandma Rose appeared oblivious to Aubrey's mental meanderings into the past. "But he's no Dr. Hunt. Still, I'd rather visit him than go all the way into Pineville."

Seeing as her grandmother's health was what mattered the most and not which doctor she visited, Aubrey relented with a weary, "Okay."

Perhaps the sorely outdated and grossly underequipped clinic had improved during the last decade. One could only hope.

DR. FERGUSON TURNED OUT to be staring fifty square in the face. But, Aubrey supposed, from her grandmother's considerably older vantage point, fifty made him a young man. And, as reported, he was competent, if a bit brusque. Aubrey could see why her grandmother didn't like him as well as his predecessor.

"You think she has strep throat?" Aubrey asked when he'd completed his exam and taken a throat culture.

"I think it's likely, given her symptoms and the fact I've treated three cases in town since last week. Here's enough penicillin to last ten days." He handed Aubrey a box containing the capsules. "Bring her back to see me next Tuesday when I return for a follow-up."

Aubrey didn't need to read a book on body language to know when she was being dismissed. "Is there any chance you can come back tomorrow? Just in case she gets worse."

"I'll be fine, Aubrey," Grandma Rose assured her.

"Aren't you a nurse?" Dr. Ferguson asked. "I thought I remember your grandmother telling me you were."

"Yes, but—"

"She couldn't have a more competent caregiver than you."

Her grandmother pulled at her arm. "Aubrey, honey, can we go home? I'm tired."

"Of course." She did look bedraggled. It was thoughtless of Aubrey to prolong the visit. "We appreciate your help, Dr. Ferguson."

"How long are you staying in Blue Ridge?"

"Another four weeks or so."

"I'm glad to finally meet you. No offense, but I hope this is the last time." He took firm hold of Grandma Rose's left arm and helped her stand. "We want your grandmother to make a speedy and full recovery without any complications."

"Thank you, Doctor," Grandma Rose said feebly, latching on to Aubrey's elbow.

The three of them shuffled outside to Aubrey's SUV. Being hoisted into the passenger seat robbed Grandma Rose of the last of her strength, and she dozed during the five-minute drive home. They arrived to find Gage's pickup truck parked in the side driveway. Like before, a circular saw had been set up on the lowered tailgate and building material was strewn across the lawn.

Aubrey attributed the flash of joy filling her to relief at having someone to help her with her grandmother and not that the someone was Gage. The argument might have held water if her heart didn't execute a full somersault at the sight of him emerging from the garage. He'd grabbed the hem of his T-shirt and was using it to wipe his face, exposing a wide expanse of flat, muscular stomach.

Spying them, he dropped his shirt and broke into a brisk walk, meeting Aubrey just as she stepped out of the SUV. "Need a hand?" he asked.

"Thank you!" Okay, some of the joy Aubrey felt really *was* relief. The trip to the clinic had exhausted her, too. "If you could help me get Grandma out of the car and stay with her while I bring the wheelchair, that'd be great."

"I have a better idea." Without waiting for her reply, Gage

strode to the passenger side and opened the door. "How about it, Rose? You ready?"

"For what?" she asked, blinking as she came more fully awake.

"A ride."

Gage slipped one arm under her knees and the other behind her back. He lifted her out of the car and carried her up the front porch steps as if she were a small child.

"I can walk, young man," she said, but her protest lacked conviction.

Aubrey dashed ahead of them and opened the door.

"Where to?" Gage asked.

"Her bedroom, please. Down the hall, last door on the right." Aubrey followed behind and watched Gage gently set her grandmother down on the bed, touched at the pains he took not to cause the older woman any discomfort.

Aubrey came up beside him. "I don't know how I would have managed without you."

"No problem."

"How about some lunch in return for the favor?"

"I've eaten, thanks. But I'll take another glass of that lemonade, if you have any."

The drawl and the grin were a potent combination, and hard to resist.

"Coming right up. Just give me a few minutes to give Grandma her medicine and settle her in bed."

It took more than a few minutes to accomplish everything and longer still to leave a message with her grandmother's regular doctor and make a pitcher of fresh-squeezed lemonade. By the time Aubrey brought Gage a tall, icy glass, a good hour had passed.

"Is your grandma doing better?" he asked, taking the glass from her.

"She's resting, finally."

"Good." He'd made impressive headway with the ramp.

"Wow! I can't believe you did all this in an hour."

He raised the glass of lemonade to his lips and guzzled almost the entire contents in one swallow. What was it with him? Did the man not know how to eat or drink like a normal person?

"I didn't do it all in an hour." He stopped to wipe his damp forehead with the back of his arm, the gesture pure Gage and cover-model sexy. "I built the ramp at home in two large pieces. Figured it would be easier and faster constructing it that way."

She smiled at his ingenuity. "It looks good."

"Care to take it for a test-drive?"

Would she ever become immune to that grin of his? "Very funny."

"I'm serious. I need to test the ramp before I bolt the pieces together. Go get your grandmother's wheelchair and ride it down."

"She pretty much uses a walker now."

"The wheelchair will be a better test."

And there would be days her grandmother might still use the wheelchair. Like today, when she was sick.

"Okay. I'll be right back." She returned shortly, pushing the wheelchair ahead of her. "Are you sure you wouldn't rather be the first one to try the ramp?" she asked Gage. "You built it, after all."

"Nah. I have less experience with wheelchairs than you do. I might crash." He stood at the bottom of the ramp. "I'll be your spotter."

Aubrey hesitated only briefly, then sat in the wheelchair and rolled it to the edge of the porch.

"Watch that a wheel doesn't go over the side," he warned. "I haven't nailed on the guards or put up the handrails yet."

The first part of the descent went without a hitch, but maneuvering the L-turn required some skill. Aubrey would have to be sure and practice with her grandmother before she left for Tucson. Her level of concentration was so intense, she didn't realize she was at the bottom of the ramp until Gage's jean-clad legs came into view.

"Hey, I did it!" She laughed. "The ramp works."

The toe of his raised work boot made contact with the wheelchair's footrest, and she came to a sudden stop. Her laugh stuck in her throat when his hands came down on the armrests, trapping her where she sat. Instantly, her Gagemeter kicked on, and she didn't have to see him to know his face hovered two tiny inches above hers.

"Look at me, Aubrey."

His low voice somehow managed to awaken every nerve ending in her body and start them tingling. Luckily, the emergency fail-safe in her brain went on red alert.

"Maybe I should go inside and ch—"

"Look at me."

Talk about manufacturing trouble where none existed. If she looked up, he'd kiss her. She knew it sure as she knew migrating birds flew south for the winter. And kissing Gage would be foolish and stupid and…and…unbelievably fantastic if their last kiss was any indication.

"I can't," she whispered, maintaining her reason, but only by a slim margin.

"Yes, you can."

She kept her eyes glued to his work boot. *Don't do it. Don't look at him.*

But then she did, and reason went the way of migrating birds.

Chapter Six

Aubrey looked up at Gage, and just like that, the control he'd fought so hard to maintain snapped. Desire crashed through him with the delicacy of a piano being dropped from a third-story window. He sucked in a breath of much needed air hoping to counter the effects. It didn't work. Nothing would work if he continued staring at her.

She had the most expressive green eyes he'd ever seen. He swore he could read her mind just by observing their subtle changes in color. Back when the two of them were married, her eyes would darken from emerald to almost hazel as he moved over her naked body, then grow darker still when he entered her. It had been—and judging by his body's reaction, still was—the most incredible turn-on.

Today, hesitation and a hint of suspicion clouded the vivid depths of those irises. She wanted him, but she was as yet unwilling to surrender to that want. Maybe she never would.

He wished he weren't so adept at this mind-reading stuff. Given the opportunity, he'd have rather gone with his first instinct and kissed her socks off. Playing it cool didn't come naturally to Gage, but he'd made up his mind she'd be the one to make the next move. Given the way he felt at the moment, he might live to regret his decision.

"You forgot to apply the brake."

"I did?"

She angled her head in question or, dare he hope, invitation. The roaring in his ears and the pounding inside his chest made it impossible for Gage to decide which.

"Uh-huh. You should apply it when you reach the bottom of the ramp." He stared at her mouth and let his eyes linger there. "You don't want to lose control and have a runaway."

"Are we talking about the wheelchair, or…" She hesitated, parted her lips, "Something else?"

She had a great mouth, too. Soft, sweet and, when she was so inclined, wonderfully wicked. He remembered the sensation of her lips trailing down his neck, his stomach, his…

Whoa, buddy, he cautioned himself. *Better not go there.* If he weren't careful, the neighbors would have one humdinger of a free show.

The threat of public shame had little effect on his raging hormones. "I was talking about the wheelchair. Did you have something else in mind?" He sure as hell did, and it involved her mouth, a place with considerably more privacy, and some *serious* loss of control.

"No." She didn't quite crack a smile but almost. Encouraged, Gage lowered his head. Seconds ticked by, then a full minute. Just when he was about to break his promise to himself and make the first move, she turned and put her lips to his ear. "Aren't you going to…"

Kiss you, his mind eagerly supplied the rest of her sentence while his muscles tensed in readiness.

"Get back to work?" Her low, throaty laugh filled his ear.

It wasn't the reaction he'd been counting on. "Yeah, right. Work."

Give credit where credit was due. The lady was good. She'd rejected him, but lessened the blow by giving him back some of the same teasing he'd given her. Gage stood and retreated a step, accepting defeat and freeing her from the confines of his arms.

"How's your family? Is your dad's gout still bothering him?" She set the brake and rose from the wheelchair, smoothly shifting the conversation from pillow talk to small talk, much to Gage's disappointment.

"Better these past couple weeks." He strolled over to his truck, which was parked a few feet away. Picking up the glass of lemonade he'd put down earlier, he swallowed the bits of melting ice cubes, then located a tape measure from the open toolbox.

"I have an article on gout and diet in the house, if you think your father'd be interested." Aubrey had followed him to the truck. "It discusses how eating the right foods can reduce the frequency and severity of attacks. I'm sure your father's doctor has already counseled him about diet, but the article details an innovative approach."

"Mom might be interested. I think she'd try anything just about now. Dad hasn't exactly been a barrel of laughs since the attacks started." Gage measured off one of the ramp guards.

"Gout is very painful."

"On everybody." He was well aware he'd let some of his resentment toward his father creep into his voice. Forcing his mouth into the shape of a smile, he said, "I'll take the article for Mom, if you don't mind. I can drop if off on my way home. She's working today."

"Your mother has a job?" Aubrey hoisted herself onto the tailgate next to the toolbox. Kicking off her sandals, she let them drop to the ground.

"Part-time. At Mountain View Realty." Gage pushed a button on the tape measure. As the mechanism sucked up the tape with a noisy whirr, he studied Aubrey. She'd sat in that exact same spot, watching him work, chatting about nothing in particular, and passing him the occasional tool more often than he could count. Old habits, he told himself. No big deal.

Yet, it felt like a big deal. She could have, *should* have, gone inside, particularly since she was determined to keep matters on a strictly casual basis between them. But she hadn't. Instead, she'd hopped onto the tailgate of his truck and dangled those gorgeous legs in front of him.

He searched in vain for the level he'd been using earlier, his mind unable to focus on much else besides…bare skin. Lots of it.

"What does she do?" Aubrey asked.

"Who?"

"Your mom. Did she get her real estate license?"

Right. They were talking about his mom's job. *Focus,* he told himself.

"No, more like secretarial stuff. Answers the phones, does the filing, runs errands. She works with Eleanor, your old friend Beth's sister."

Aubrey nodded. "Does she like it?"

"She likes it a lot, and I think it's been good for her to get away from the ranch."

Very good.

Gage saw the dulling effects decades of hard physical labor had on his mother's once cheerful personality. Working outside the home restored a small measure of it.

"And your dad? He's okay with your mom working? If I remember, he was sort of…old-fashioned."

"No." A derisive chuckle escaped before Gage could stop it. "He hates it."

But he sure didn't hate the extra income, thought Gage. There had been a few weeks during the worst of the drought season when Susan Raintree's paycheck had been the only thing putting food on the table.

"After our ranch was chosen to participate in the grazing study, Dad tried his best to get Mom to quit." This time, Gage's chuckle rumbled with genuine mirth. "She refused."

"You and your dad getting along better?" Aubrey dug around in the toolbox beside her and came up with the level, which she passed to Gage.

How had she known what he was looking for? Old habits, again, no other explanation for it.

"We're not fighting. As long as I don't get called to a fire, we manage to stand each other's company."

They didn't talk for several minutes while Gage went over to the ramp and measured for the handrails. Pulling a carpenter's pencil from his back pocket, he jotted the different lengths he'd need on a scrap piece of wood.

"What's Hannah up to these days?" Aubrey asked when he returned.

"Taking summer classes at Pineville College. She's getting her degree in agricultural management."

"Good for her! She's always loved ranching."

"Yep. And she'll be able to use that degree when she takes over for the old man."

"Hannah's going to manage the ranch?"

"So she says."

Aubrey broke into a sunny smile. "And with her taking over, that leaves you free to be a firefighter."

"*Will* leave me free. She has another year and a half to go before she graduates, possibly longer." Depending in part on the family's finances, Gage added silently. He picked through the stack of two-by-twos on the ground beside the truck.

"The Raintrees are actually going against tradition." Aubrey shook her head in disbelief. "Who'd have believed it?"

"Well, not all traditions. Dad still has trouble with Mom working."

"But not your sister?"

"Apparently, a woman taking over the family business is okay, but holding a job outside the ranch is not okay. Yeah," he continued before she could comment, "the rest of us have a little trouble with the distinction, too." He laid the two-by-twos on the ground, one next to the other, sorted by size.

"When do you sleep?" Aubrey's green eyes narrowed on him, more thoughtful than critical

"At night, usually. Like most people."

"Seriously, Gage. The ranch doesn't run itself. Someone has to cover for your mom working part-time, your sister going to college and when your dad has a gout attack. Process of elimination leaves you."

"It's not as bad as you think."

"What about your firefighting?"

"What about my firefighting?" Her line of questioning reminded him too much of the arguments he had with his father. On the plus side, it took his mind off her legs.

"Does anyone do the chores while you're gone or do they accumulate?"

"The chores get done, sooner or later." Some days, a lot later.

If they had an extra couple hundred dollars to spare, he'd hire Kenny Junior for a week. But there never seemed to be an extra ten dollars lying around, much less two hundred. Hannah's summer school costs had depleted the family expense fund. Gage's hazard pay was being used to build it back up in preparation of the fall roundup when they'd have no choice but to hire help.

"You forget," Aubrey said. "I lived on your ranch for six weeks, I know the work is never ending. No one person can do it all in without sacrificing something. I figure it's sleep. Tell me I'm wrong."

"I get enough sleep." And he did, if one considered four to six hours a night enough sleep. Maybe he should risk his father's wrath and push Hannah to help more. She didn't offer unless asked, using school as an excuse to avoid pitching in.

"If you don't take care of yourself, you'll wind up sick, or dead from exhaustion."

"Okay, Nurse Stuart. I promise to get more sleep if it'll make you happy."

"Joke if you want," Aubrey snapped.

He heaved a long sigh.

"I'm sorry." She was immediately contrite. "It's not my place to tell you what to do."

"Forget it. I'm used to bossy women. I was married to one once."

She picked up a screw and threw it at him.

"Hey!" He ducked, and the screw glanced off his shoulder.

"I admit I'm bossy. But only because I care about you."

He was tempted to ask how much she cared, but held his tongue. "Thank you."

"Which reminds me." She planted her fists on her hips in a classic pose. "What the heck are you doing here anyway?"

"Building a handicap ramp?"

She scowled at him. "You're busy. Can't one of the other volunteer firefighters build it?"

"I want to help your grandmother. You're not the only one in town who cares about her."

"I know, but—"

"Dad's having a good day. He's handling the chores while I'm away. And if you quit your nagging, I'll be finished in another hour. Then I can go home and get some of that sleep you insist on."

He reached out and cupped her chin in his palm, his fingers stroking her cheek. The gesture was automatic, something he'd done often when they were younger to shut Aubrey up and not hurt her feelings.

Old habits again, and apparently impossible to break.

Their gazes connected, and something akin to the sweet rush of emotion that once lit up their lives passed between them.

The moment lasted only until the phone rang from inside the house.

"That's probably Grandma's doctor. I called him earlier." Aubrey hopped off the tailgate and slipped on her sandals. "I'll be right back." She dashed toward the house.

"I'll be waiting."

Gage watched her until the screen door slammed shut behind her before returning to work, already missing her company and counting the minutes until she returned.

She didn't, however, come right back. An hour dragged by, during which Gage did all he could on the ramp and then some. Eventually, he ran out of excuses to stay. From the periodic snatches of muted conversation drifting through the screen door, he knew she was still on the phone.

Who could she be talking to for so damn long? Not her grandmother's doctor, that was for sure.

A boyfriend maybe? Gage's gut turned to stone. He'd assumed because she hadn't remarried, she was unattached. But what if her reluctance to get involved with him again was because she had some bozo in Tucson on the string?

Venting his frustration on his tools, Gage chucked them into the back of his truck, missing the toolbox more times than not. The debris followed the way of the tools. Within a few minutes, his truck bed resembled a war zone. The ruckus had the neighbor, Mrs. Payne, popping out onto her porch for a look-see, but not Aubrey. She stayed inside.

He was just climbing into the truck when he decided to say goodbye before leaving. Opening the screen door, he hollered, "Hey, in there, I'm leaving. See you later."

Aubrey materialized in the doorway leading to the kitchen, a portable phone stuck to her ear and a grim expression on her face. "Oh, okay. See ya later. And thanks."

Gage tromped back to his truck, his mood decidedly sour. He took some pleasure in the knowledge that if Aubrey were indeed talking to a boyfriend, the conversation wasn't going well.

AUBREY CLOSED the medicine cabinet in her grandmother's bathroom, shut off the light and padded through the bedroom toward the door.

"Good night, dear." Her grandmother's tired voice traveled to Aubrey from across the darkened room.

She paused, a hand resting on the doorjamb. "I thought you'd be asleep already."

"Not quite."

Her grandmother had rallied after her long afternoon nap, and the two of them ate a light dinner together in front of the TV. Neither were hungry, her grandmother because of her strep throat and Aubrey because of her terse phone conversation with her father.

Shortly after dinner and not long into *Wheel of Fortune,* a flushed and feverish Grandma Rose retired to bed. Aubrey hoped the antibiotics would kick in soon.

"I assume the call with your father didn't go so great." The bedsheets rustled as Grandma Rose changed positions.

"How'd you guess?"

"I woke up a couple times and heard bits and pieces of your conversation."

"Was I loud?" Aubrey retraced her steps back into the room.

"No, dear. You weren't loud." Grandma Rose patted the edge of the mattress, and Aubrey obediently sat down. "But you looked a little downtrodden during dinner. Care to tell me what's wrong?"

"Nothing's wrong." Nothing *new,* at least. Not keen on discussing her father, Aubrey attempted to divert the conversation. "Annie was there, visiting the folks. She and some friends just got back from a trip to L.A. Guess they tried out for some reality television show."

During the fifteen minutes she'd spoken with her younger sister, Aubrey learned more than she cared to about the audition process. In many ways, she envied Annie and her free-spirited, take-life-as-it-comes attitude. Being the serious, overachieving firstborn had its drawbacks.

"Sounds just like Annie," Grandma Rose said with amusement. "Did she and her friends make it onto the show?"

"They won't find out for a few weeks. Mom sends her love and says to drink lots of fluids." After Annie, Aubrey had talked with her mother. "She was upset to hear you have strep throat, but glad to know you're making such excellent progress with your physical therapy. I promised I'd call her tomorrow with an update on how you're doing. I would have brought you the portable phone if I'd known you were awake."

"That's all right. I'll talk to her tomorrow. How's your father doing?"

Grandma Rose might have been physically weak, but she

was mentally sharp as a tack. There was no way Aubrey was going to get out of talking about her father. Everyone said she and him were too much alike. They frequently knocked heads, although even in the midst of their most heated confrontations, Aubrey understood her father loved her and only wanted what was best for her.

"He's fine and concerned about your recovery."

"He didn't want you to come here. He wanted you to stay in Tucson."

"No, Grandma," Aubrey instantly protested. "That's not true."

"Yes, it is. I haven't been his mother-in-law all these years for nothing. I can read him almost as well as your mother. Where you and your sister are concerned, anyway."

Aubrey expelled a long sigh. She would have rather lied but found it impossible. "You're right. He did want me to stay in Tucson. Not for the reasons you think," she hurriedly added. "He loves you and would have hired the best possible nursing care for you."

"You're the best possible nursing care I could ever want or need." Grandma Rose linked fingers with Aubrey, much like she had when Aubrey was little. "So, tell me, why didn't he want you to come?"

"It has to do with Uncle Jesse and Aunt Maureen's deaths."

She sensed more than saw her grandmother's sorrowful expression.

"They were such lovely people. Good friends of your parents."

"You know I was on duty the night of the accident when they were brought in?"

"Your mother told me. She said you took it pretty hard."

"Yeah, I did. Mom and Dad were in Chicago at a seminar. I hated giving them the news on the phone, but I didn't want them hearing it from a stranger."

It felt good to finally talk with someone about that night. As an E.R. nurse, Aubrey had become accustomed to setting her emotions aside. It was, she'd found, the only way to survive a job where heartache and tragedy were a daily occurrence.

"I was shocked when I recognized Jesse and Maureen beneath all the blood, and, well, I panicked briefly." In truth, she fell into a stupor. "It took me a couple seconds to compose myself." She'd stood like a stone statue until another nurse grabbed her by the arm and shook her.

"It's amazing you were able to function at all. That speaks very highly of your skill and dedication."

"Maybe."

"How can you think otherwise?"

"Because since that night, I've suffered three more… moments of indecisiveness." Aubrey looked down at her lap.

"Oh, you poor thing."

"Grandma, I'm afraid." Tears pricked Aubrey's eyes. "If I can't overcome this problem, I might have to quit the E.R. and change my specialty to something where I'm not required to treat accident victims."

A very long, very silent pause followed. Aubrey's laugh verged on desperate.

"Say something, will you?"

"What does your mother think of your situation?"

"I haven't told her."

"Can I ask why?"

"Dad feels the fewer people who know, the better." It had occurred to Aubrey her father might be ashamed of what he perceived as a failure.

"Well, he may be right," Grandma Rose said reassuringly.

"He wanted me to stay in Tucson. Face my problem head-on." Not run away like she had in college. "And I can see where he's coming from, even if I don't agree."

"I have no doubt after a short break from the E.R., you'll return to work and this difficulty you're having will become a thing of the past."

"And if not?"

"You go into another specialty," Grandma Rose said simply.

But it wasn't so simple for Aubrey. "I don't want to go into another specialty."

She could cite any number of reasons: the training she'd had, the certifications she'd earned. The plain truth was she thrived on the fast-paced environment of the E.R. Her aspirations were to one day manage the emergency department of a large metropolitan hospital. Oh, sure, she could find a modicum of enjoyment in other fields of nursing, but would she find the same satisfaction?

The desolation filling Aubrey abated, and some of the determination her grandmother had been talking about rushed in to take its place. "Maybe Dad was right and coming here was a mistake. I should be at work. Not hiding out in Blue Ridge."

"You're going back to Tucson?"

Aubrey heard her grandmother's panic and quickly reassured her. "I promised you I'd stay for six weeks. But afterward, yes. I have to go back. You understand, don't you?"

"I do." Grandma Rose lowered herself onto her pillow. "Will Gage?"

The question, from out of left field, gave Aubrey a start. "I'm sure he will."

"And if he doesn't?"

"It really makes no difference."

"He's still in love with you, Aubrey."

Okay. She hadn't seen that coming, either. "We're friends is all." Did friends usually flirt and kiss?

"And *you're* still in love with him."

"I am not!"

"Hmmm," was Grandma Rose's only comment.

Aubrey collected her thoughts and tried to put them in a semblance of order. "We were married once and, yes, in love for a long time before that. There are bound to be lingering feelings."

A lot of lingering feelings. If her grandmother, a sick, elderly woman, had noticed, it was worse than Aubrey realized. She really had to keep Gage at a distance, not encourage him as she'd done today.

"After you, work is my number-one priority," Aubrey said with conviction. "Whatever it takes, I'm going to overcome this freezing problem."

"You will. What you went through, seeing someone you love die in front of your eyes…" Grandma Rose's voice thinned and trailed off. "Takes a body a while to get over it."

Her grandmother would know, having been at her grandfather's side when he'd passed away in the hospital.

She found and squeezed Aubrey's hand again. "I'm so proud of you, sweetheart. Always have been. You'll survive this ordeal and be a better nurse for it in the long run."

Tears pricked Aubrey's eyes anew; tears of sentimentality rather than sadness. She was glad she'd come to Blue Ridge, especially glad she'd had this talk with her grandmother. It made all the recent disagreements with her father fade into nothingness.

"You're tired." She stood and rearranged the mussed bedsheets. "It was wrong of me to keep you up."

"I'm glad you did."

"So am I." Aubrey kissed her grandmother's cheek. "But you need your rest. It's the only way you'll get better."

"Good night, sweetheart. See you in the morning."

Aubrey closed the door on her way out and shuffled across the hall to her room. It had been a trying day from beginning to end, her emotions all over the place. Tomorrow, when her mind was clear and her body refreshed, she'd address the problem with Gage. If she didn't take immediate steps to tone down their highly charged attraction, her leaving in another four weeks would wind up a carbon copy of the last time, complete with hurt and anger.

Unfortunately, thoughts of Gage refused to be put off until tomorrow. After tossing and turning for a good half hour and mashing her pillow into an unidentifiable lump, Aubrey got up and prowled the quiet house, stopping first to peek in on her grandmother.

The hall clock told her it was past ten. A cool breeze wafting in through the screen door convinced her a breath of fresh air might be just the ticket to calm her jangled nerves. Aubrey switched on the porch light. Outside, the breeze followed through with every tantalizing promise it had made, sifting through her hair and caressing the parts of her not covered by the gym shorts and tank top she'd worn to bed.

She went to the far end of the porch and leaned against the column. Eventually, she relaxed, lulled by chirping crickets and a pair of hooting owls. Both nature's symphony and her respite came to an abrupt halt when a pair of headlights swung into her grandmother's driveway, accompanied by the sound of spitting gravel.

"Who in the world…"

Pushing off the column, she walked tentatively toward the porch steps. She wasn't worried. Being Blue Ridge and not Tucson, her late night visitor was, in all likelihood, no stranger.

The vehicle, a large, looming shadow in the moonless night, came to a stop behind Aubrey's SUV. The headlights flicked off and the driver's side door opened. A lone figure emerged—tall, broad-shouldered and undeniably male.

Aubrey's heart recognized Gage long before her brain did and beat wildly in anticipation.

So much for toning down their highly charged attraction.

Chapter Seven

Gage stared his fill. He wasn't the kind of person to hurry a good thing, and Aubrey in shorts and a tank top was one incredibly good thing.

"I lost my cell phone earlier," he stammered. "I think it might have fallen off my belt while I was working."

He stood at the bottom of the porch steps, Aubrey at the top. Their positions put him on direct eye level with her breasts. With her back to the light, he couldn't see much. Imagination and memory filled in the blanks.

"Oh." She hugged her waist. "I can't help you much, I haven't been outside until just now."

"Do you mind if I have a look around?" Given the fact he hadn't been able to tear his gaze away from her, his remark could have been construed differently.

"Go right ahead. Do you need a flashlight?"

"I brought one." He produced a miniflashlight from the back pocket of his jeans.

Neither of them moved. "Gage," she began, then faltered. Lifting her arm, she brushed back the hair from her face. One breast raised and strained against the fabric of her pajama top.

"Uh-huh?" His attention remained fixed on her. She was more sexy, more beautiful in that moment than he ever remembered.

"About today…" She rubbed the back of her neck.

Gage watched, his mouth dry as an old bone baking in the hot sun. She let her arm fall, and he narrowly avoided groaning with frustration.

"I'm leaving in another four weeks and returning to Tucson."

"Okay." He knew that and wasn't sure he liked it.

"It's uh…" She shifted her weight to her other foot and blew out a breath. "It's probably a good idea for us to keep a little distance between us. Just to avoid any problems when the time comes for me to leave."

Gage moved forward until he was toe to toe with the bottom porch step. "You think we'll have problems when you leave?"

"Possibly… Yes," she said with more confidence.

He returned the flashlight to his jeans pocket and climbed the bottom step. His new position put him on eye level with her mouth. Not a bad place to be, either. "Why?"

"Because…" She swallowed nervously, her strength apparently deserting her. "We have a lot of history together and shared memories."

Gage sensed a brush-off coming and refused to go down without a fight. "A lot of *intimate* history."

"Well, yes."

From his raised vantage point, he had a great view of her cleavage. "And you don't want to start anything we can't finish, right?"

"Exactly."

"No."

"What?"

"I said no." He leaned closer, inhaled the freshly showered scent of her. "I, for one, want to start something with you, and I'm pretty sure you want to start something with me, too. But you're scared and understandably so."

"You're wrong." Her protest sounded weak, thank God.

"About you wanting to start something, too, or you being scared?"

"Gage, please."

"Tell me something, Aubrey. When I had you trapped in the wheelchair this afternoon, did you want to kiss me? Not *would* have, but *want* to?"

"I…uh."

Gage eased forward and angled his head upward as if to meet her lips. He stopped a few inches short. "Yes?"

If he turned his head marginally to the left, his mouth would graze the underside of her jaw. He resisted. For their relationship to develop into something more, Aubrey had to stop being a participant and start being the initiator.

"The truth, Aubrey. No more games." He closed the distance between their mouths by several more millimeters. "Do you want to kiss me?"

Her breath hitched. "You don't fight fair."

"Not where you're concerned."

"Fine," she said with what sounded like forced resignation. "I want to kiss you. Will you leave now that I've confessed?"

"No way."

"How come?" Her brow furrowed in surprise and then indignation. "Because I won't kiss you?"

"Because I haven't found my phone." He chuckled and moved closer still. "And because you haven't kissed me."

"If that's what it takes to get you to leave…" She dipped her head, bypassed his mouth and brushed his cheek with her lips.

Gage went completely motionless, waiting.

She didn't pull away. Good, but not enough. Difficult as it was, he kept his arms locked at his side, silently pleading for her to end his torture, either by going inside or giving them what they both wanted. Seconds stretched into an eternity.

At last, she cradled his cheeks in her hands. "Happy?" she crooned and pressed her mouth to his smile.

"Ecstatic." His tongue traced the outline of her bottom lip as his arms circled her waist.

"This changes nothing. We're not getting involved." She tilted her head back as he tasted the silky column of her neck and the hollows above her collarbones.

"Quit your jabbering and give me a real kiss."

She obliged him by fully fusing her mouth with his.

Since she'd technically instigated the kiss, he let her control it. He had no complaints about the arrangement and, evidently, neither did she. They started out slow, familiarizing themselves with each other through tender and tentative explorations—something they'd missed out on during their frantic kiss at the community center.

Their leisurely pace didn't last, however. Aubrey slid her hands from his face to his shoulders, pulling him to her. Gage took her invitation a step further. Without separating their mouths, he lifted her off her feet, walked up the remaining two porch steps and stumbled blindly in the general direction of the lawn chairs.

They almost made it.

A shrill chirping sounded from a distance. "Dammit," he grumbled and set Aubrey down, though he didn't release her.

"What's that?" she asked dazedly.

"My cell phone."

"Your cell phone?"

"I told Hannah to call the number in thirty minutes. I figured I could follow the ringing to the phone."

Aubrey disengaged herself from his arms and straightened her pajamas. "You'd better go find it while it's still ringing."

"Yeah." He could see the change coming over her. Already, she regretted kissing him, possibly questioned her momentary loss of sanity. The chances of them picking up where they left off once he found his phone were slim to none. "I'll be right back," he said and beat a path to the front yard.

Flashlight in hand, he followed the sound of the chirping, which quit as he was closing it on it. Gage was considering asking Aubrey to go inside and call the number for him when he found the phone near the ramp. He picked it up and hooked it to his belt. Only then did he look for Aubrey.

She stood near the screen door, one hand on the knob.

He walked to the porch, ready to put up a fight. She wasn't going inside without first talking to him. At the top step, he paused.

"Aubrey—"

She silenced him with a raised hand. The other one clutched the doorknob like a lifeline.

"I'm not ready for this, Gage. As tempted as I am to be with you, I can't. I'm leaving soon, and it wouldn't be fair to either of us."

At least she admitted to being tempted.

"You could always stay."

She shook her head. "I have my job to consider."

He understood. In a town the size of Blue Ridge, employment opportunities on a whole were limited and virtually nonexistent for nurses. He could hardly ask her to give up her career for him. Not when he resented his father for making just such a demand. And even if Aubrey were willing, she'd come to resent him, too.

"More importantly," she said, "there's a…situation I've been ignoring that needs resolving."

He had no right to ask, but nonetheless, did. "A boyfriend situation?"

"No." She shook her head, her green eyes a little lost. "Work and family."

"I'm sorry." Gage's apology was sincere. He well knew the obstacles of balancing work and family. "Anything I can help with?"

"This is something I have to deal with on my own."

"Sounds serious."

"It is." Eyes closed, she massaged her forehead. "I'm having a bit of a career crisis, I guess you could say. And my dad and I don't exactly agree on how I should handle it."

Gage knew Alexander Stuart regularly attempted to impose his will on his daughters, Aubrey in particular. Funny, where their parents were concerned, she and Gage really were very much alike.

"If you ever want to talk, I'm a good listener."

"Thanks. Maybe another time. It's getting late and I have an early morning." Opening the door, Aubrey stepped inside. "Good night, Gage." Her face was a dark shadow behind the screen. "Thanks for building the ramp. You're a good friend of the family."

He started to say he could be a whole lot more than a good friend if she'd let him but kept his mouth shut. Pressuring her for more before she was ready would only reverse the tentative inroads he'd made. And besides, he was coming away with considerably more than just his cell phone.

At least he now understood a little better what was bothering Aubrey and how it was contributing to her case of cold feet where their relationship was concerned. He just didn't know what to do about it.

Yet.

"See ya later."

Gage bounded down the porch steps, digging his keys from his pocket when he hit bottom.

No doubt about it, Aubrey still cared for him. If she didn't, the thought of getting involved wouldn't scare her like it did. And most importantly, she didn't have a boyfriend. At least one who mattered.

For the first time since her return, Gage felt like he had a fighting chance with Aubrey.

"More mashed potatoes, honey?"

"Thanks, Mom." Gage accepted the serving bowl from his mother's outstretched hands and ladled a second helping onto his dinner plate.

He wasn't particularly hungry but didn't want to hurt his mother's feelings. She'd spent half the afternoon in the kitchen laboring over their meal. Neither was he particularly talkative. None of the Raintrees were, which was a little unusual. Then again, they were all pretty tired.

Hannah, a notorious chatterbox, had stayed up late the

previous night doing homework then gotten up at the crack of dawn to leave for class. For his part, Gage had ridden out bright and early to check the water level of the stock tanks and round up any strays. His father, enjoying a second straight week free from gout, had come along. Too proud to admit he'd overextended himself, he was paying the price in the form of sore muscles and aching joints. Gage's mother, evidently weary of trying to jump-start family mealtime conversation, settled for seeing that everyone got enough to eat.

Gage's excuse wasn't as much fatigue as his inability to keep Aubrey and the searing kiss they'd shared last night off his mind. He still didn't know if he should be mad at his sister for interrupting them, or thank her for doing so. Chances were good if she hadn't called his cell phone when she did, Gage and Aubrey would have yielded to their impulses and given new meaning to the word *reacquaint*.

He need only close his eyes to recall the feel of her as she came into his arms, warm and lush and, for a few heart-jarring moments, willing. If Gage didn't know better, he'd think he was seventeen all over again.

"Peach pie anyone?" his mom asked, getting up from her chair and reaching for her husband's empty plate. "It's homemade."

"You sit, Mom," Hannah said. "Gage and I will get the dishes and serve dessert. Won't we, big brother?"

"Absolutely." Anything to stop thinking of Aubrey. Gage snatched the platter of leftover roasted chicken from the center of the table.

Outside, Biscuit barked, announcing the arrival of a vehicle in the Raintree driveway.

"Who could that be?" his dad demanded and hobbled toward the door.

"Bring some extra pie," his mom called to Hannah in the kitchen. "We have company."

Gage's cousin, Chase, entered the great room behind

Joseph, cradling his seven-year-old daughter, Mandy, in his arms. One of her feet was bare, and she was whimpering.

"Sorry to barge in on your dinner," Chase said, visibly distressed. He turned in a half circle as if he didn't know quite what to do with his daughter.

"What's wrong?" Gage asked and went toward them.

Chase wasn't one to fluster easily, or hadn't been until he'd become a single dad six months earlier when his wife—make that his ex-wife—walked out. The change in family structure had turned him into a chronic worrier where Mandy was concerned.

"She was playing out behind the shop and cut her foot on a piece of sharp metal. It's deep, but I don't think she needs stitches. I was hoping you could have a look and give me your opinion."

"Sure." Gage led the way to the kitchen.

"She's had such a rough go of it lately," Chase said as they walked, "I hate to put her through any unnecessary trauma."

In the kitchen, Gage patted the end of a long counter inlaid with colorful ceramic tile. "Sit her down here why don't you."

"Hi, Mandy, honey." Hannah, who was serving up the last of the pie, greeted them. "What happened?"

The little girl clutched a tattered stuffed toy to her side and sniffled. "I hurt my foot."

"Aw, that's too bad. Well, Uncle Gage will fix you right up."

"I don't want no stitches."

"Who does?" Hannah licked a dribble of pie filling from her finger.

Gage pulled a chair from the breakfast set over to the counter and sat down in front of Mandy. He tickled the back of her ankle and when she automatically lifted her leg, he deftly captured her foot in his hand.

Mandy giggled. "Quit it, Uncle Gage."

"What have we here?" He removed the bandage Chase had put on the cut and tsk'd as if her injury was something awful

to behold. "I say surgery's in order. What about you, Dad?"
He looked to Chase for confirmation.

She squealed and tried to jerk her foot away. "No!"

"I'm kidding, pumpkin." He tickled her ankle again, glad
to see she wasn't in a lot of pain. "It's not so bad. I'm sure a
butterfly bandage will be enough."

"You don't by chance have any?" Chase asked. "I'm out."

"Not here. Maybe at the station. We could ride over and
dig through the first-aid supplies." Gage reexamined Mandy's
cut. "Has she had a tetanus shot recently?"

"When she started kindergarten. I called SherryAnne
before we left the house." Chase's flat answer discouraged
any further questions about his ex-wife. "What about antibiotics? Do you have any of those at the station?"

"Just topical." Gage reapplied the bandage. "But I agree
she should have some. Lacerations on the foot are prone to
infection."

"I don't want a shot." Mandy's bottom lip protruded in a
pronounced pout, and her eyes brimmed with tears.

"No shot," Gage said. "Just some bad-tasting medicine."

Mandy scrunched up her face but didn't object.

"Doc Ferguson won't be back in town until Tuesday."
Chase gathered his daughter in his arms. "Maybe I should
take her to the E.R. in Pineville after all. I'll call you tomorrow and let you know how it went."

"You won't get home until ten or later," Hannah said.
"Stay and have some pie with us. You can leave in the
morning."

"I have appointments all day." Chase was a veterinarian,
the only one for thirty-five miles in any direction.

"Maybe Mom can take Mandy," Hannah suggested.

"She's working tomorrow." Gage stood and returned the
chair to the table.

"Thanks anyway." Chase headed out of the kitchen with
Mandy in his arms. "But it's probably better for everyone if
we just go tonight."

"Wait." Gage reached for his cell phone. "I have an idea." He hit a speed dial number on the key pad and waited while the call went through.

"Hello."

A small jolt of anticipation went through him at the sound of Aubrey's voice. "Hi, it's Gage. Are you busy at the moment?" He winked at Mandy. "I have a patient who requires the services of a good nurse."

AUBREY LEANED her back on the front door of the clinic and shielded her eyes against the setting sun. In the distance, Gage's pickup truck rumbled down the road, headed straight for her. Grandma Rose had insisted she'd be fine alone for a short while, leaving Aubrey with no legit excuse to refuse Gage's request.

Not that she would have refused to help Chase and his daughter.

She'd met Mandy only once, at her grandfather's funeral. Mandy had been a toddler then, Chase and SherryAnne happily married. Aubrey liked Gage's older cousin, though she hadn't known him well and SherryAnne hardly at all. During her summers in Blue Ridge, Aubrey's attention had been fixed exclusively on Gage.

The truck swung into the drive and parked beside her SUV. Both doors opened and Gage emerged from the driver's side. He paused, his bare arm resting on top of the open door.

His searching gaze landed on Aubrey where it remained. She could feel the effects of his intimate scrutiny clear to her toes. A very small, very wistful sound escaped her lips, and for one fleeting moment, she considered disregarding every one of her resolutions about Gage.

"Thanks for agreeing to see us."

Chase appeared by Aubrey's side, intruding upon her and Gage's interlude—for which she was grateful. Something went haywire with her reasoning every time she found herself near Gage. It was a distraction she didn't need, especially while working.

"Hi, Mandy." Aubrey smiled at the little girl in her father's arms, clinging to both him and a velveteen pony for dear life. In a cheery voice, she said, "I bet you don't remember me. You couldn't have been more than two when we met."

Mandy answered by burrowing her face in her father's shirt.

"Don't be shy," Aubrey cooed and moved closer.

"I hate shots," came a muffled reply.

"Want to hear a secret?" Aubrey uttered the last part in a conspiratorial whisper. "So do I."

One eye peeked out and peered at Aubrey. "But you're a nurse."

Aubrey shrugged. "Doesn't mean I like shots."

The eye went back into hiding.

"You know what?" Aubrey was acutely aware of Gage as he passed by. She tried her best to hide the current of sensation winding through her. "Because I don't like shots, I'm real gentle when I give them. The patients at the hospital took a vote, and they said of all the nurses, my shots hurt the least."

The eye reappeared. "Is that really true or are you just making it up?"

"Well…" Aubrey scrunched her mouth to one side and squinted. "A little of both, maybe."

The eye crinkled, and Aubrey suspected Mandy might be enjoying the teasing. She pivoted to face Gage, who was unlocking the clinic door.

"You have a key to this place?"

The dead bolt gave, and he pushed open the door. "Yeah, the volunteer fire department works closely with the clinic."

Aubrey supposed that made sense. Just like she supposed Gage had received some EMT training.

"You understand I can't dispense antibiotics to Mandy without Dr. Ferguson's consent?"

"Give me just a minute." Gage walked into the clinic and went straight to the phone sitting on a scarred metal desk that was more junk than antique. He referred to a list of phone numbers taped to the desktop and dialed.

Aubrey stowed her purse on the counter. "Let's see about that foot." She gestured toward the narrow examination table.

The little girl was loathe to leave the sanctuary of her father's arms. He finally got her to sit on the table but not without a fuss.

Aubrey bent down to inspect Mandy's foot. "I promise I won't touch you, sweetie, unless you tell me it's okay. Agreed?"

Mandy nodded, her mouth compressed into a tight bud.

"All right, hold your foot up so I can see it."

She complied and, after more coaxing, allowed Aubrey to remove the bandage.

Halfway through her examination, Gage got Dr. Ferguson on the line. "He'll talk to you."

Aubrey went over to Gage and took the phone from him. His fingers lingered on hers far longer than necessary.

"H-h-hello, Dr. F-Ferguson." She gripped the phone tight to counteract the sizzling effects of Gage's touch.

"Hello, Aubrey. I wasn't expecting to speak to you again so soon. How's your grandmother doing?"

"She's better." A brief update on Grandma Rose gave Aubrey a chance to compose herself. Afterward, she filled in the doctor in Mandy.

"Give her some cephalexin." He told Aubrey where the prescription medicines were stored. "Would you mind writing up a short report for me before you leave and putting it on the desk?"

"Not at all. Thank you, Doctor."

"Thank you. This has been a great help to me." For once his voice was warm. Almost friendly. "I've no right to ask but would you perhaps consider volunteering at the clinic one or two afternoons a week? I could really use someone with your skills."

"I…" Aubrey's refusal stuck in her throat.

In all honesty, she missed practicing nursing. Treating minor injuries and checking sore throats might not compare to the fast-paced environment of Tucson General's E.R. and the addictive rush of adrenaline, but she'd no doubt enjoy herself. And heaven only knew the shabby little clinic could use a strong administrative hand.

From the corner of her eye she watched Gage talking to Chase. Could she handle something else that would put her in close contact with Gage? Doubtful. Nor did she need more ties to Blue Ridge—ties that would be hard to cut when the time came to leave.

"Aubrey?" asked Doctor Ferguson.

"I'm sorry. I got sidetracked." *And how.* She swallowed before speaking. "As much as I'd like to volunteer, I'm afraid I can't. I'm leaving the end of the month and would hate making a commitment only to break it." She noticed Gage watching her and averted her head. Hadn't she done as much to him when they were young—made a commitment and then broke it?

"I understand." Doctor Ferguson's voice was once again clipped. "If you change your mind, give me a ring."

"I will."

Aubrey disconnected after saying goodbye. Expelling a long sigh, she spun around—and found herself nose-to-chest with Gage. When had he moved? Bracing a hand on the edge of the desk saved her from losing her balance and falling straight into him.

"Is everything okay?" he asked, giving her not one spare inch of space in which to maneuver.

"Fine."

"You sure?"

It was obvious he wanted to ask her about her conversation with Doctor Ferguson, and he might have if not for Mandy.

"Am I gonna get a shot?" Huge, worry-filled eyes pleaded with Aubrey.

"No, sweetie. I promise." Aubrey reassured her with a big smile. "And no stitches, either. But I'm going to have to wash your foot real good and put some medicine on it that might sting a little."

The little girl hugged her stuffed pony to her like a shield.
Aubrey sympathized, wishing she, too, had a shield to protect herself from the man standing in front of her.

Chapter Eight

Gage flung the spark-plug wrench he'd been using into the toolbox at his feet, swore in frustration and contemplated what kind of trade-in value he could get on the old tractor. Forty-five back-breaking minutes in the sweltering sun and he still hadn't figured out why the worthless piece of junk kept stalling out.

Yeah, right. Who was he kidding? The Raintrees could barely afford a new wheelbarrow much less a new tractor.

Climbing onto the front wheel, he leaned down and poked around the engine for the umpteenth time, hoping to identify the problem before his knees and his patience gave out.

He had his right arm buried up to his shoulder in the bowels of the engine when his cell phone rang.

"Great," he growled, straining to reach a loose wire that hopped about with a life of its own. "Who could that be?"

As he reached around with his left hand to unclip his phone from his belt, it suddenly hit him how much he sounded like his father.

The thought took him aback. Way, way aback.

Before he could answer his phone, the radio on his belt emitted a series of tones. Instantly, Gage's heart rate accelerated to Mach speed. He hopped off the tractor wheel and, listening to the radio, sprinted to the house.

By the time he reached the back porch, his phone had

stopped ringing. Ignoring the number on the caller ID, he called dispatch.

"We have a fire," the voice said upon answering his call. "Seventeen miles northwest of Saddle Horn Butte."

"Where do I report?"

He was given the various details of the fire and the meeting location for his crew. Not bothering to stop for a pencil and paper, Gage committed the information to memory as he tore through the kitchen, gathering his keys and wallet. Anything else he needed was stored in a metal container in the bed of his truck. Within minutes, he was behind the wheel.

He didn't make it to the end of the driveway.

His father hobbled toward him from the side yard, hollering and waving his arms. "Where are you going?"

Gage slammed to a stop and rolled down the window. "There's a fire," he called out. "I just got the call."

"What about the tractor?"

"I'll finish repairing it when I get back."

"And when exactly will that be?"

"I don't know."

"You can't just leave." Joseph reached the side of the truck. He was panting slightly. "We need the tractor to move those boulders blocking the lower access road."

"The access road's been blocked for months. Another few days won't make a difference."

"Kenny Junior's coming tomorrow to help dig post holes for the new fence. He can't get his truck past those boulders."

"Not now, Dad." Gage started to roll up the window.

"Hold it right there, young man." Joseph jabbed the air with his index finger. "Your first duty is to this family. Fighting fires is something you can do in your spare time."

"And when do I ever have any spare time around here?"

Countless trees and brush were being destroyed while Gage and his father argued. Possibly summer homes and recreation sites. Ranches and grazing land by the acre. Gage couldn't wait any longer. He let up on the brake, and the truck rolled forward.

"I'll call when I have a minute."

"You leave now, you might as well not come back." Joseph's scowling expression could have been carved from stone.

"Is that an ultimatum?"

"Yes."

"Whatever." Gage was in no mood for idle threats.

"I mean it this time, son."

Did he? Gage didn't think his father was any more serious than the last two times he'd issued similar warnings.

But Gage was—serious as a heart attack. He wasn't just a firefighter these days, he was up for promotion to crew leader and not about to ignore his increased responsibilities.

"Be careful about giving ultimatums, Dad. You might not like the answer you get."

Joseph's jaw went slack, then clenched.

Gage peeled out of the driveway and barreled down the road. More than one rabbit and lizard saw him coming and executed a mad dash for safety.

At the main gate leading into the Raintree Ranch he met up with Hannah who was returning from the college. He debated stopping to chat with her and decided he had thirty seconds, and thirty seconds only, to spare.

She shoved open the gate, the rusty mechanism objecting with a high-pitched squeal. "You were going fast enough." She walked over to lean on Gage's open window. "Where's the fire?"

"Northwest of Saddle Horn Butte."

"Oh, wow!" Her face registered shock. "I was just kidding."

"I don't know how long I'll be gone. Sorry to dump everything on you."

"Don't sweat it."

"Dad's in a bitch of a mood."

"What else is new?"

"He's mad because the tractor's still not working."

"I'll get Kenny Junior to look at it when he comes out tomorrow."

He had no doubt Kenny Junior would move a mountain for her if she so much as batted an eyelash at him.

She rapped the side of his truck. "You get a move on. We'll be fine."

"Thanks, sis." Some of the weight on his shoulders lifted. "I appreciate you taking care of things while I'm gone."

"Hey, it's cool. That's what family's for." She waved him off. "You be careful, you hear?"

Gage hit the gas. A glance in his rearview mirror told him Hannah was already in her car and on her way home. Good. If anyone could cajole their dad out of his bad mood, it would be her.

He didn't realize until he reached the highway that Hannah had never before offered to handle things for him while he was at a fire. She was usually too caught up in her own little world to think beyond personal wants and wishes.

Maybe his younger sister was finally growing up.

And if that were the case, his life might have just become a tiny bit easier.

"YOU SHOULD REALLY have that looked at by a doctor." Aubrey laid an ice pack on the Hotshot's knee. The joint was swollen to half again its normal size. She'd had to cut a hole in his pants to get at it. "You probably tore a ligament."

He lifted the ice pack and inspected the soft bulge where his kneecap should be. "I'll be fine."

Aubrey had insisted he elevate the injured leg and used one of the metal folding chairs in the community center as a prop. She handed him two ibuprofen and a bottle of water.

"Take these."

"You have anything stronger?"

He *was* in pain, she thought, and not nearly as tough as he tried to appear. "Not here and not without a doctor's orders."

"It's okay." He downed the tablets. "I want to be clear-headed if they call us for another shift."

She gave him a wet washcloth, and he used it to clean his

face and hands. The rest of him would have to wait. With one bathroom and twenty Hotshots wanting to shower, he had a good two hours to kill before his turn came.

"You're not thinking of going back to the fire?" Aubrey asked, not quite believing her ears.

He lifted one shoulder in an indifferent shrug.

"Put too much pressure on that knee and you could cause permanent damage to the ligament."

"It's just a sprain." He dismissed her concern in favor of a plate of spaghetti, courtesy of another volunteer.

Aubrey shook her head in dismay.

She'd treated a dozen Hotshots for minor to moderately serious injuries in the last two days and not one of them even remotely considered calling it quits. They were either raving lunatics or the bravest individuals she'd ever met.

"Hey, Aubrey," her friend Eleanor called. "Can you run next door to the Wash-o-matic and pick up that last load of laundry?"

"Sure." It would be her fourth trip of the day. Aubrey would hate to count the number of bath towels, dishtowels, bedsheets, rags, tablecloths and assorted clothing she'd washed and folded.

As she crossed the large room to the main door, her gaze gravitated toward the TV, where a reporter was broadcasting live a few miles from the fire. Smoke filled the sky behind her, a swirling, billowing mixture of white and gray. The news, however, was encouraging. At last report, the fire was sixty-five percent contained. Experts predicted it would be ninety-five percent contained by morning.

So, why hasn't anyone heard from Gage?

When Aubrey showed up at the community center the day before with a food donation, she told herself it was the neighborly thing to do. It was the same excuse she used when she returned that morning and then stayed all day. In truth, she'd been hoping for information on Gage, who'd been gone three days without a single word.

She tried not to concern herself. After all, Gage was an

experienced firefighter, and they'd been receiving regular updates on his crew via radio transmission. At least, that's what Kenny Junior told Aubrey earlier when he dropped off some planks to finish the handicap ramp.

And it wasn't like she and Gage had a relationship or anything. They were friends. Period. Friends and former spouses.

So, did former spouses go around kissing each other like they were crazy in lust?

No point denying it. She *had* kissed him, *wanted* to and *did* it. Gage might have egged her on, but he hadn't coerced her. Not by a long shot. What must he be thinking? One minute she'd told him they needed distance in order to avoid problems when she left town. The next minute she was kissing him like she couldn't wait to jump naked into bed with him.

Aubrey grabbed the empty laundry basket and trudged out the door into the deepening light of early evening. The Wash-o-matic was a short hop, skip and jump from the community center. Just far enough to work up a sweat.

While dumping clean laundry from the dryer into the basket, she asked herself, not for the first time, why she'd returned to the community center, not once but twice, and why she was doing exactly what she'd told the Sierra Nevada captain she wouldn't—namely, help out.

The answer, she knew, had as much to do with being useful as it did with finding information on Gage. Aubrey missed her job, plain and simple. Though an entirely different environment, there were similarities between a busy E.R. and the community center.

Both hummed with excitement and energy, not to mention that they both existed in a state of constant tension. The highly trained and dedicated staff members were united in a common purpose: bringing comfort and relief to the people who walked through the door. Aubrey may have been a stranger to most people in the room, but she felt right at home, and they sensed that about her.

Was that the reason Gage and the other Hotshots fought fires? Did they have the same desire—no, compulsion—to help those in need as Aubrey and her coworkers?

Maybe she'd been wrong. Maybe she did understand what motivated Gage. But nursing didn't usually require one to risk their life on a regular basis as firefighting did.

She stood, slamming the dryer door shut. Where was Gage? Why didn't he call? Balancing the basket of clean laundry on her hip, she made her way back to the community center.

In her absence, a mud-splattered minibus had parked near the front entrance of the community center. The last of its occupants, a man wearing brown pants and a navy blue T-shirt, slipped through the door. Aubrey's step faltered. Those were the colors of the Blue Ridge Hotshots. Had Gage's crew finally returned?

Running while carrying a full laundry basket proved cumbersome, but Aubrey didn't drop so much as a sock. Not that she would have stopped to pick it up.

Inside the community center, she quickly scanned the new arrivals, searching for Gage. Her chest heaved, and her temples pounded. From the back and side, all the Hotshots looked alike; their damp hair mussed, their clothes rumpled and every inch of them streaked with grime and soot.

Aubrey wove her way through the large room, her eyes going from one to the other. Smiles greeted her. Not one, however, belonged to a familiar face. Damn! Where was Gage? The emblems on the navy blue T-shirts identified the firefighters as Blue Ridge Hotshots. His crew. He had to be with them, didn't he?

She went up to the nearest one, moving the laundry basket to her other hip. "Excuse me. Did Gage Raintree come back with you?"

He gave her a curious and then appreciative once-over. "Are you Aubrey Stuart?"

"Yes." How did he know her name?

A smile lit his sun-burned and wind-reddened face. "Nice

to meet you. I'm Marty Paxton, Gage's captain. I've heard a lot about you."

"Nice to meet you, too." She shook the hand he offered, more interested in news of Gage than social pleasantries. "Can you tell me where Gage is?"

"I can do better than that." His smile grew. "I can show you."

Relief swept through Aubrey, followed by anticipation. The one-two punch left her wobbly in the knees. "Okay."

Marty raised an arm and pointed at the open doorway leading to the kitchen. "In there."

The laundry basket hit the floor with a thud. Deep laughter followed Aubrey as she darted through the maze of folding tables and chairs blocking her route to the kitchen. She assumed the laughter was Marty's. The hell with him. He could think what he wanted, she didn't care. So long as she confirmed with her own eyes that Gage was safe and in one piece.

He was standing at the sink, his right hand under the faucet, water running full blast. Eleanor stood beside him and stared at his hand, her lips thinned in concentration.

They both glanced up as she skittered to a stop. Gage's expression conveyed surprise. Eleanor's didn't. In fact, her eyes twinkled with an I-thought-so mirth.

Aubrey dismissed her as she had Marty. What did they know anyway?

"Hey."

"Hey."

Eleanor reached around Gage and shut off the water. "Titillating as this conversation is, I'm afraid I simply must tear myself away."

"Huh?" Gage turned to look at her. "Sure. Thanks, Eleanor."

"You're welcome." She smirked at Aubrey on her way out. "To both of you."

Aubrey didn't remember deciding to throw herself at Gage the second Eleanor left the kitchen, yet somehow she wound up in his arms.

"Thank God you're all right." Her voice hitched with emotion. "I got worried when no one heard from you."

Gage could have gloated, she supposed. He could have told her he knew all along she was lying and still had feelings for him no matter what she said, but he didn't. Instead, he squeezed her tight as if he couldn't bear to be parted from her ever again. Aubrey's heart sang.

"I was worried about you, too," he murmured into her hair.

Though she would have gladly let him, he didn't attempt to kiss her.

"Why didn't you call?" she demanded when they finally broke apart.

"Sorry. I would have if I'd known you wanted to hear from me. Did you want to hear from me, Aubrey?"

"Yes." The admission came out softer than she intended.

"Seems to me you made it pretty clear the other night at your grandmother's house you wanted to put some distance between us."

How could she explain her reasons to him when she didn't understand them herself?

"I talked with your mother this morning at the real estate office," she said, avoiding his question. "You haven't checked in with your family, either."

"They know where I am."

"But they don't know you're safe."

"I'll call later."

She'd obviously struck a sore spot with him and let the subject drop. "How's the fire? I heard earlier it was sixty-five percent contained."

"It's closer to eighty now."

"Wow. That's great news. When do you report back?"

"We may not have to. We're supposed to stick around here for the next few hours just in case." He cradled his left hand inside his right one.

Aubrey's nurse's eyes zeroed right in. "What happened to your hand?"

"Just a small burn."

"Let me see."

He obediently placed his hand in hers, and she gently uncurled his fingers. His palm was bright red. Blisters the size of dimes covered the pads of each finger, including his thumb. A single large blister an inch long cut across the center of his palm. Charred particles were imbedded in the skin alongside the blisters. It had probably looked worse before he washed it.

Aubrey took a second to compose herself. "How did this happen?"

"I got a sticker or some damn thing inside my glove. It hurt like a son of a bitch. I took the glove off for just a second to get whatever it was out. Right about the same time this burning log decided to roll down the hill at us."

"And you had to stop it," she said, turning the cold water back on and sticking his hand under the flow. She didn't release his wrist.

"Actually, Ernesto stopped the log. Not intentionally. He tried to jump clear of it but tripped and was knocked flat on his butt. The log rolled onto his legs."

"Oh, my God, Gage."

"I didn't think and just reached down to shove it off him."

"Is he all right?"

"Yeah. They took him to Pineville hospital. He may need plastic surgery." Gage indicated his injured hand with a nod. "This is a scratch compared to him."

"This is hardly a scratch. You have second-degree burns."

Aubrey pictured a burning log rolling down a hill toward Gage and went ice cold, inside and out. She had to fight the debilitating numbness threatening to turn her limbs into dead-weights and reminded herself she wasn't in Tucson General's E.R. No one's life hung by a thread, depending on her quick responses to save them.

She clenched her jaw and tried to concentrate on the present. Enough was enough, she chided herself. This ridiculous nonsense had to end, and soon. She was a nurse. A professional. Someone who—

"Aubrey? What's wrong?"

"Nothing."

"You don't look very good."

"I'm fine," she said, drawing deep, even breaths. The infusion of extra oxygen helped warm her frigid blood. "Just tired."

"Me, too."

"I bet you are." Feeling a little better, Aubrey shut off the water and wrapped Gage's hand in a clean towel. "Let's dress this for you."

She led him out of the kitchen and toward the folding table that served as the first-aid station.

"Why are you here?" he asked as they walked.

"I'm volunteering."

"Since when? I thought you didn't want to make any commitments only to break them."

"It's just for today." And yesterday. She didn't inform him that one of the main reasons she'd returned to the community center was to learn if he was safe. "Have a seat." She motioned to an empty chair.

"I have a better idea." A mischievous grin deepened the lines of fatigue bracketing his mouth.

"What?" Aubrey sensed a wild scheme about to be hatched.

"Grab what you need, and let's ditch this place."

"To go where?"

"I'll show you."

She shook her head. "You need to rest."

"That's exactly what I have in mind." The gleam in his eyes far from instilled her with confidence.

"Let me take you home," she insisted.

"I'm not going home. Not yet." The finality of his statement left no room for argument.

Aubrey again pondered what had happened between Gage and his family, but curbed her curiosity for the moment.

"Please." He flashed her the same woeful expression that

had broken her resolve so often when they were younger. "It's not far. I promise."

"Okay." She gathered up the medical supplies she'd need, ignoring the warning bell clanging inside her head. "On one condition."

"Name it."

"You agree to see Doctor Ferguson first thing in the morning and have him check out your hand."

"I'm fine. It's no big deal. I've had rope burns worse than this."

"Gage."

"All right. If I'm not called back to the fire."

"You can't go back with your hand like th—"

He cupped her cheek in his palm, effectively silencing her—something he'd also done often when they were younger. "Quit being a nurse for one hour, okay?"

"Okay." She didn't correct him. Her concern for his well-being had little to do with her profession and a lot to do with her much-denied-but-there-nonetheless feelings for him. "What about food? Are you hungry?"

"Starving."

"There's some leftover pizza in the fridge. I'll get us a couple slices. And something to drink."

This time, Gage took the lead. As promised, they didn't go far. Just next door, to the volunteer fire department station. Only they didn't enter the station as Aubrey anticipated. He took her out back, and the sight that met her caused her to screech to a grinding halt.

Parked in the shade of the building stood a motor home. The same one they'd resided in during their short marriage. Memories inundated Aubrey, one after the other, in rapid-fire succession. Some were heartwrenching and agonizing, others tender and sweet and incredibly wonderful.

She gulped, unable to move.

"Come on," Gage urged, taking her elbow with his good hand.

Did he have any idea what he was asking of her?

"Give me a second." She seriously considered making a beeline straight back to the community center as fast as her legs could carry her.

Going inside the motor home with Gage wouldn't be wise. She'd be inviting trouble on the grandest of scales. When it came to Gage, she was far safer surrounding herself with as many people as possible. Something always seemed to happen—something that involved mouths and bodies coming together like high-powered magnets—every time they were alone.

But he was hurt, she reminded herself. And in pain. Tired, hungry, battered and bruised. He probably had nothing more dangerous in mind than a nice long nap. Right?

Her feet remained glued to the ground.

"I figured we could talk in private while you bandaged my hand."

Talk in private?

She wasn't reassured. Talking with Gage inevitably left her feeling like an emotional dishrag.

Her gaze traveled between the motor home and Gage and back to the motor home. Aubrey had a vivid recollection of Susan Raintree helping her sew curtains for the many little windows. Were the curtains still hanging? The exterior had taken a serious beating from the elements. If the inside in any way resembled the outside, the motor home should have been condemned years ago.

"Come on," Gage urged again. Quietly. Beseechingly. Seductively.

She let his voice slide over her, and the small shiver that coursed through her as a result wasn't unpleasant. If anything, it was tantalizing.

A momentary flash of insight penetrated Aubrey's fog-filled brain. She was, she realized, at some sort of turning point in her relationship with Gage. She either went back to the community center and the situation remained status quo:

a constant state of sexual tension flowing between them that would continue until the day she left Blue Ridge. Or, she accompanied him into the motor home, a course of action that pretty much launched them on a path from which there was no turning back.

Did she want to be with Gage badly enough to risk an agonizing separation when she returned to Tucson? And what about him? Could he handle a repeat of what happened ten years ago?

"I'm leaving at the end of the month," she said in a choked whisper.

"So you've told me."

"Nothing that happens today or any day between now and then will change my plans."

"I know."

"Do you?"

"Yes."

She studied his face for several long seconds and saw that what he said was true. He was indeed resigned to her eventual leaving.

"All right." Aubrey squared her shoulders and took a tentative step forward. "We can talk."

Climbing the steps of the motor home was like walking through a time portal. She placed her hand on the doorknob and pushed. In an instant, the last decade faded away. Her skin prickled, her toes curled and her pulse drummed. Gage coming up behind her worsened her strange symptoms. Entering the small and achingly familiar domain, she had the distinct impression talking wasn't all they'd do, especially when she glimpsed the faded curtains hanging from crooked rods.

Chapter Nine

Gage strained not to move as Aubrey treated his injured hand. Every touch of her fingers, every brush of her arm, elevated his sense of awareness to a higher level. He hadn't brought her to the motor home in an effort to seduce her, but seducing her was pretty much all he could think of at the moment.

"Gage?"

"Sorry. Did you say something?" He tried to recall her question, but his brain function had been reduced to zilch.

She sighed and delicately probed a blister. "I said, you really should be taking antibiotics. Dr. Ferguson can prescribe one for you when you see him tomorrow."

Gage tensed, though not from pain, and reminded himself to breath regularly. She definitely wasn't lying to Mandy when she told the little girl the patients at Tucson General voted her the gentlest nurse. Aubrey's careful ministrations, combined with her proximity, pushed him to the very limits of his tenuously held control.

He sat at the compact dining table, the sole available seating in the motor home. Only one of his long legs fit in the cramped space beneath the table. The other one stretched across the narrow walkway, the toe of his boot butting the front panel of a lower storage cabinet. Aubrey barely had room to maneuver, which accounted for their constant—and he assumed unintentional—physical contact, along with his fast-growing state of arousal.

Gage wriggled in the seat and tugged on a pant leg.

"Does that hurt?" Her worried glance flitted to his face and then back to his hand.

"Not at all. I'm just a little stiff."

"I bet you are."

She had no idea.

"Is your shoulder bothering you? I noticed you rubbing it earlier."

"A bit."

"I brought some liniment." She inclined her head at the assortment of medical paraphernalia lying on the table.

A pain-relieving cream probably wasn't going to help Gage with what ailed him. If anything, Aubrey massaging liniment into his sore muscles would only increase his discomfort. Nonetheless, he picked up the tube with his left hand and attempted to unscrew the cap—*attempted* being an apt description. Gage was anything but ambidextrous.

"Here. Let me." Aubrey relieved him of the tube. "Take off your shirt."

Gage rose, inadvertently crowding Aubrey.

She lowered her gaze, watching him unbuckle his belt. He watched her watching him, and deliberately slowed his movements, hoping for a reaction.

"Do you need help?" she asked.

He figured he could succeed one-handed, but where was the fun in that? "Sure, thanks."

He raised his arms over his head, and Aubrey whisked off his shirt. Unfortunately, she did it like a nurse undressing her patient and not like a woman stripping her lover.

So much for wild, crazy fantasies coming true.

What, Gage wondered, did she think about the two of them being there together? Did she want him as much as he wanted her?

"Sit," she ordered.

He plopped back down in the seat. Aubrey came to stand in front of him, squeezing a dollop of liniment into the center of her palm. The outside of her thigh pressed lightly against the inside of his. Her movement appeared innocent, much as Gage wished she had an ulterior motive. One sign, one teeny tiny sign from her and...what? Throw her on the floor and take her right there?

She soothed the liniment into his shoulder using strokes that were strong, competent and incredibly gentle. Gage closed his eyes, hovering midway between heaven and hell. He silently pleaded for her to stop while simultaneously hoping she'd go on touching him until dawn tomorrow.

He got his first wish.

"Is the water connected?" She turned and moved to the sink.

"Last I checked." Gage had run a garden hose and extension cord from the station so that the motor home would have, if not all the comforts, at least the minimum necessities of home.

She flipped on the faucet. Water sputtered and spit before flowing in a steady, albeit thin, stream. After washing and drying her hands, Aubrey picked up a box of sterilized gauze pads.

"I'm not sure the best way to bandage your hand." She narrowed her eyes contemplatively. "You don't by chance have an old glove hanging around we could use?"

"I'd like to shower first. Get out of these filthy clothes."

"Oh." She caught his stare and something flickered in her eyes, giving his innocent comment an entirely different meaning.

Gage responded with a rush of heat that made the fire he'd been fighting the past three days seem like a marshmallow roast.

They'd showered together often in this motor home. He recalled in minute detail the sight of her bare skin glistening beneath the spray of hot water and the enjoyment they'd both derived from him toweling every inch of her dry. Seeing her cheeks flush, he thought he might have finally broken through the barrier of her professional demeanor.

"I should go," she said in a controlled voice. "Give you some privacy."

Before she could execute the backward step she obviously wanted to take, Gage reached out with his good hand and grabbed hers. "Stay."

"I can't. I…shouldn't."

His thumb toyed with the band of her wristwatch, burrowing under it and worrying the sensitive spot on the inside of her wrist. She was leaving soon, very soon, returning to the career she loved and the life she'd made for herself in Tucson. He had no business whatsoever starting something with her, especially when he had nothing better to offer. Yet he couldn't bring himself to let her walk out of the motor home.

"I won't pressure you into anything you don't want or aren't ready for, Aubrey. I swear."

"I know. And that's just it." She squeezed her eyes shut and gave a small, nervous laugh. "You wouldn't have to pressure me."

There was no thinking involved. No moment of indecision. Gage came out of his seat like a rocket. In the next second, he had Aubrey pinned against the counter.

Green eyes met his, an array of emotions flaring in their smoky depths. Surprise. Curiosity. Arousal. Nothing to indicate displeasure or unwillingness. It was all the invitation he needed.

"I'm filthy." He bent to nuzzle her cheek and ear. "And I stink."

"So I noticed." Sighing, she linked her arms around his neck. Her breasts fit snugly against his chest, and Gage could discern her taut nipples through the fabric of her shirt. He longed to tease them with the tips of his fingers or, better yet, the tip of his tongue.

"Take a shower with me."

She wrapped an ankle around his calf and adjusted her hips to align with his.

"Will we still fit?"

"Hell, yes." He'd find a way or die trying.

Mouths meshed and tongues tangled in an explosive, heat-generating kiss that left them both shaking and short of breath. He fumbled with the top button of her shirt, desperate to be skin to skin with her. Body to body. Soul to soul.

With a smile both coy and shy, Aubrey brushed his hand aside and unfastened the buttons herself. She didn't stop there.

Giving her room to maneuver, Gage eased backward until his behind hit the table. He would have liked to participate in her undressing, but his injured hand pretty much prevented that. No matter. Standing idly by and watching Aubrey shuck out of her clothes wasn't exactly torture.

Then again, maybe it was.

She paused, one finger hooked beneath the strap of her skimpy pink bra. A rumble of desperation emanated from his chest. Had she changed her mind? He hoped not. Almost as much as he hoped his radio wouldn't go off for at least an hour or so.

"Do you have any protection?" she asked.

She hadn't changed her mind. *Thank you, God.*

"Uh, yeah. I think so." He dove through the door to the bathroom and snapped on the dim overhead light.

An unopened box of condoms sat on the medicine cabinet shelf, and he could have cried with joy. His foot caught on the doorjamb in his haste to exit.

"Sorry." He offered a half smile in way of apology for his clumsiness.

Her eyebrows lifted. Not so the corners of her mouth. "You keep condoms in the medicine cabinet?"

Gage realized how sleazy he must look to her. "These are Kenny Junior's," he hurriedly explained. "They've been here for I don't know how long. When I first moved the motor home to the station, he planned to use it for a bachelor pad."

"Kenny Junior?" Aubrey cracked a smile, and they both burst out laughing. The volunteer firefighter had the heart of a teddy bear and a physique to match. She eyed the box of condoms speculatively when their laughter finally died. "Are they still good?"

Gage held the box in a death grip and read the label. His sharp burst of laughter bordered on giddy. "They don't expire for another six months."

Aubrey tipped her head to one side. "Okay."

"Really?" The single word hardly summed up everything he was thinking and feeling, but coherent sentences were beyond his present capabilities.

"Yes, really."

Her smile was warm and genuine and filled Gage with an elation he hadn't felt in years. Ten years to be exact. She sauntered toward him, picking up where she left off and easing the straps of her bra down her shoulders. He dropped the box of condoms on the table and opened his arms.

Like the teenagers they'd once been, they tumbled into the bathroom. The remainder of their clothes landed in a heap on the floor. Gage cursed his inept hand more than once.

"Take it easy." Aubrey reached inside the shower and adjusted the spigot. The ancient plumbing squeaked and gurgled before releasing a sputtering spray. "You'll hurt yourself."

In that moment, a thousand needles could have pierced Gage's flesh and he wouldn't have noticed. Aubrey was exquisite. All feminine curves and angles in exactly the right proportions.

She spun around, and her wide eyes followed a path from his face, down his chest, and then lower. There, it lingered. Gage couldn't hide his very obvious desire for her, nor did he try.

"Water's taking a sec to heat up," she said in a thready voice.

"We can wait." He made the offer strictly for Aubrey's sake. A dip in the Arctic Ocean wouldn't diminish his ardor, much less a little cold water.

"I'd rather not." Her eyes met his again and she moistened her lips.

The dozen or so inches separating them instantly diminished to one. Pushing the plastic curtain aside, he scooped her up in his arms and deposited her in the shower. Water pelted her, collecting in rivulets and streaming down the length of her body to pool at her feet. He stared, mesmerized. She was so incredibly beautiful.

"Aren't you going to join me?"

"In a minute."

"Gage." She laughed self-consciously and reached for the plastic curtain.

"No way." He stopped her before she pulled it closed and climbed into the shower with her.

There was enough room for the two of them if they stood plastered against each other, an arrangement that suited Gage just fine. He wrapped his arms around Aubrey's waist, liking the feel of her slick, wet skin sliding along his. He'd missed this, missed her, more than he let himself admit.

Before he could kiss her, she picked up a sliver of pink soap from the recessed dish and rubbed it in her palms until a frothy lather dribbled between her fingers. She spread the lather over his shoulders and chest and across the flat plane of his stomach. Repeating the process, she washed his hips and thighs. Gage didn't dare move, anticipating her next move.

To his surprise and pleasure, she cradled his cheeks in her hands and washed his face and neck. The sweet, tender treatment of his sunburned skin affected him far more greatly than any bold strokes in more intimate places might have.

"My turn," he said after rinsing his face beneath the spray and then snatched the soap from her slippery fingers.

Rotating her around so that they stood with her back to his front, he rubbed the soap back and forth over her breasts until they were covered with suds. He paid special attention to the plump undersides before focusing exclusively on her nipples.

"You don't have to." She sighed contentedly as he continued soaping her with his uninjured hand.

"Try and stop me." He had plans, and they included giving better than he got.

He traveled down her belly, making large, sweeping circles with the soap, and eventually ended at the junction of her legs. She parted her thighs and let her head loll back into the crook of his neck.

"Do you want me to touch you?" he asked, nibbling the side of her neck and fitting his erection into the cleft of her buttocks.

In answer, she moved her hips.

"Say it," he urged.

"Touch me. Please, Gage. I'm going crazy."

She wasn't the only one.

He dropped the soap, reached between her legs and began exploring. His left hand didn't possess the dexterity of his right one, and he cursed it. Showing no hesitation whatsoever, she covered his hand with hers and gently guided him. Her lack of inhibition was such a turn-on, he very nearly lost it then and there.

Aubrey hadn't climaxed their first several attempts at love-making. They were both too young and inexperienced. Fortunately, sex improved as the weeks passed. Gage was an apt student, paying careful attention to what she liked. He put his learning to good use now, adding the patience he'd acquired as a grown man. The results were incredible.

"Like that?" he croaked when she arched her back and moaned seductively.

"Just like that."

When the first tremor took her, he wrapped his right arm around her middle and held on for the ride. He didn't loosen his grip until she fell limp against him.

"Let's get out of here," he suggested.

Without waiting for her answer, he turned off the spigot, ripped open the shower curtain and grabbed a towel. Laying it across her shoulders, he stepped out of the shower, then helped her do the same. Gage then had the enjoyment of toweling Aubrey dry. It was as much fun as he remembered.

She giggled when he knelt and picked up her foot to dry her toes. "What about you? Is there another towel in here?"

"I don't need one."

Most of the water on his skin had already evaporated due to extreme temperature—*his* internal temperature, not that of the motor home. Sensing her watching him, he glanced up.

"That was nice," she said in a throaty whisper.

Not sure whether she was referring to the shower, the toweling off or her climax, he said, "I enjoyed it, too."

"Hurry." Aubrey spun sideways and dashed out the door.

Gage chased after her, grabbing the box of condoms as he flew by the table. She got only as far as the overhead bunk before he caught her. Considering her impish grin, that may have been her plan all along. He boosted her into the bunk before crawling up after her. Laughing, they fell onto the sagging foam mattress.

"Just like old times." She toyed with a lock of his damp hair, twirling it between her fingers.

"Better." He kissed and nibbled her lips. Lightly. Playfully.

Their mood turned serious when Gage rolled Aubrey onto her back and positioned himself over her. He removed a condom from the box before tossing it in a corner. Extracting the condom from the foil package with his left hand defeated his abilities.

"I'll do it."

Aubrey not only opened the package, she placed the condom over his erection. She didn't hurry, testing the very limits of his willpower. When she at last finished, he settled himself between her legs, looked into her eyes, and watched them darken from emerald to hazel. It was like coming home after a too long absence.

"Make love to me, Gage." She elevated her hips in an urgent plea.

"Aubrey. Oh, God."

She *did* want him. Every bit as much as he wanted her, and

Gage was able to put their uncertain—if not impossible—future from his mind. For the moment, at least. Today, she was his. He'd worry about the consequences tomorrow.

AUBREY TOOK A SMALL BITE of food and grimaced. She wasn't a fan of cold pizza, but eating gave her something to do while Gage inhaled his meal. She washed the cheese-and-pepperoni combo down with a swallow of soda, wondering how to start a conversation and when. They really needed to talk, which was the reason they'd come to the motor home in the first place. More so now that they'd made love. But Gage also needed to eat and sleep.

Maybe she should wait for another day.

"You okay?" He caressed the back of her hand, a tentative smile on his face. "You seem a little preoccupied."

The rumpled, just-flopped-out-of-bed look gave him a sexy edge that would be difficult for any woman to resist, especially one who'd finally accepted she was starting to fall for him all over again.

"I'm fine." She smiled back, also tentatively.

They sat across from each other at the small dining table, knees knocking and feet scuffling. While Aubrey had dressed in the bathroom, Gage scrounged up an old pair of jeans from the bottom of the closet. No sooner were they dressed than an awkward tension descended upon them. It had yet to ease. Talking, Aubrey mused, might only increase the tension.

And not talking is going to relieve it?

The metallic crunch of an aluminum can being compressed jarred her from her reverie. Gage leaned over, opened the cabinet under the sink and deposited his trash in the plastic container stored there.

"You done?" He reached for her soda.

"Not yet. Thanks."

Aubrey still had half her pizza slice left and most of her drink, which she was reluctant to give up. Picking at the remains of her food would give her something to do while they talked—that was if they ever got around to talking.

Damn. She really needed to say something. Gage might have…expectations…given the manner in which they'd spent the last hour. Unrealistic expectations.

Screwing up her courage, she blurted, "This changes nothing. No matter what happens, I'm—"

A shrill chirping cut her off. Gage's cell phone. He lunged for the bathroom where he'd left his dirty pants on the floor. Aubrey wasn't so much frustrated at the interruption as she was worried that Gage might be called back to the fire. She'd yet to bandage his injured hand.

"Raintree here," he said from the bathroom, slightly out of breath. "Yeah, Marty." A pause. "No, I didn't leave. I'm in the motor home." Another, longer pause. "All right. I'll stick around for a while just in case." He emerged from the bathroom, the phone wedged between his shoulder and ear. "No problem. Thanks for calling." Disconnecting, he dropped the phone on the dining table. "Looks like we've been relieved of duty."

"That's good news." And it was. For Gage, for the thousands of wilderness acres spared and for the people living near Saddle Horn Butte. Aubrey pushed away the remains of her meal. "Let's finish bandaging your hand."

Doing something routine might put them—put her—at ease enough so they could converse comfortably.

She operated by rote, applying an antibiotic ointment and bandaging the tip of each finger. A break in the conversation didn't come, mostly because there was no conversation.

Now or never, she told herself and opened her mouth to speak.

Gage beat her to it. "Do you remember our secret spot?"

"Sure I do."

He grinned. "And the day we found it?"

"How could I forget?" She fitted a gauze pad over the blister on his palm and taped the dressing in place. "I still have a scar from your fishhook."

"That was the first time I kissed you."

"I seem to remember it was me who initiated the kissing. You were all freaked out over a little blood."

"I wasn't freaked out." His grin went from amused to sly. "It was an act to trick you into kissing me."

"You're terrible." She shot him an appalled look, entirely feigned.

"That was also the place where we first made love." His voice dropped in volume. "Then decided to elope right afterward."

Her hands stilled, as did her breathing and, she was relatively certain, her pulse.

"Gage…"

"Don't you freak now. I'm not going to suggest we elope again."

"Good." The single word came out on a rush of relief.

"But I do have feelings for you." His tone was reassuring and reasonable, two things she didn't feel at the moment. "And I think you have feelings for me, too. I know you, Aubrey. You wouldn't have made love with me if you didn't."

He was right, of course.

"What do you want from me?" she asked. More importantly, what was she willing to give?

He cupped her chin in his bandaged hand. "I'd like for us to try and make a go of things for the remainder of your stay in Blue Ridge."

"A go of things?" she asked hesitantly. "As in boyfriend and girlfriend?"

"Yeah. Pretty much."

Aubrey mulled this over with amazing calm, considering her chaotic frame of mind. She supposed she could blame their sleeping together today on raging hormones trapped in close, familiar quarters. Or nostalgia, even. But dating Gage? Dinner at her house Friday night and a movie in Pineville Saturday afternoon? That would involve a conscious decision, one she might eventually regret.

"What if we do make a go of things? What happens when it's time for me to leave?"

"We'll figure something out. Find a way to be together."

"Oh, Gage." He could be so sweet. So optimistic. The complete opposite of Aubrey, who tended to anticipate trouble around every corner. "It's not that simple."

"You have a job, I know."

"Not just a job, a career. One I've worked hard for. As have you."

"Okay." He nodded jerkily. "So we compromise. Tucson isn't the only place with a hospital. Pineville has one. Granted, it's not as large."

Aubrey rubbed her temple, though it was her chest that really hurt. "If it were merely a matter of me finding another nursing job, I'd say yes. But there are other factors to consider. What about your obligation to your family's ranch?"

"Hannah's taking over in another year and a half. Two at the most."

"Which means you can't move to Pineville until she's graduated college."

Tightly thinned lips were his only concession to her point.

"There's another reason I need to go back to Tucson General. One I haven't mentioned."

He waited for her to enlighten him, one eyebrow quirked.

Aubrey hesitated, worried he might view her as incompetent once she revealed her problem. She took pride in her skills and abilities, and her periodic freeze-ups had carved a huge hole in her confidence.

"You remember our family friends, Jesse and Maureen Donaldson?" she started out slowly. "They died a few months ago in an automobile accident."

"Your grandmother told me. I never met them, but you talked about them a lot and I know you were close."

"I was on duty the night they were brought into the E.R." She paused, waiting for the lump in her throat to shrink enough for her to continue.

"Oh, jeez. I'm sorry, sweetheart. That must have been awful for you."

"When I recognized them, I froze. It was like my brain stopped communicating with the rest of me. While they lay there, dying, I did nothing."

"You were in shock."

The prickle of impatience she felt was directed at herself, not Gage, but it was him she snapped at. "An E.R. nurse can't afford to be in shock."

"Okay."

"Sorry." She was instantly contrite. "This is hardly your fault."

He accepted her apology with a shrug. "So you're human like the rest of us."

She shook her head. "When you work in a large metropolitan E.R., someone you know and care about is bound to be brought in eventually. You have to be able to detach yourself from any personal involvement until the crisis has passed. I didn't detach myself," she finished on a miserable note.

"There's not a firefighter I know who hasn't had a moment of indecision, including myself."

"A moment of indecision isn't the same thing as a complete inability to respond." She lifted his injured hand and turned it over, palm up. "When that burning log rolled onto your friend's leg, did you hesitate? No. You acted on instinct and did what was necessary to save him without regard to your personal safety."

"Ernesto's life wasn't hanging by a thread, either."

"Would you have reacted differently if it had been?"

"I hope to hell not."

"I only wish I could say the same thing and with as much conviction." Unshed tears stung her eyes. Staring out the small window over the sink didn't dispel them. Neither did Gage's compassionate tone.

"I remember feeling like I was walking underwater," she

continued. "Everything was blurry and wavy. Sounds ran together. That's never happened to me before, and I've seen some truly terrible things."

She stopped for a ragged breath. "Neither Uncle Jesse nor Aunt Maureen regained consciousness, which I suppose was a blessing. Aunt Maureen died first. Her neck broken."

"That's awful."

"What if it's my fault Uncle Jesse and Aunt Maureen died?" She choked, trying to regain her composure. "How many moments were lost while I just stood there, doing nothing? Moments that could have been utilized to save their lives."

"Their deaths weren't your fault," Gage said adamantly. "They were beyond saving. I know it sounds cruel, but a few minutes, a few hours, wouldn't have made a difference."

"But what about the next time I freeze up?" The ball of misery inside Aubrey's chest expanded until it pressed against her lungs, cutting off her air supply. "And the next?"

"How often has it happened?"

"Often enough."

"When was the last time?"

"Oh…" She glanced at her watch. "About seven o'clock. In the kitchen when I saw your hand."

"You didn't freeze up."

"No. But I had a serious panic attack."

"Which you obviously conquered."

"Covered, not conquered." She turned toward him, fear welling inside her. "I'm scared, Gage. Scared I won't be able to practice emergency nursing ever again."

"Would that be so bad?"

"How would you feel about having to give up firefighting because you couldn't handle the pressure?"

"I'd hate it and be angry with myself for being such a wimp."

"Exactly." Gage had hit the nail squarely on the head. She *was* angry with herself. Flat-out furious. "I have to go back to Tucson when my leave of absence is up and face this problem. If I don't, I might lose my nerve altogether. Dad thinks I shouldn't have left in the first place."

"He's not always right."

"True." Had Aubrey not been so well acquainted with Gage, she wouldn't have detected the trace of bitterness in his voice. "But in this instance, he may be." His hand still lay near her arm, and she clasped it gently. "I'm going back, Gage. I have to. Please understand."

"I do. I care about you, remember? And I'm behind you 100 percent." He brought her fingers to his mouth and kissed the knuckles. "But I still want to see you while you're here."

"I couldn't take a repeat of the last time I left. My heart isn't up to the stress, not after the beating it's had the last couple of months."

"No strings. I promise."

"You're not exactly a no-strings kind of guy."

"I won't make a stink when you leave."

She believed him, or maybe she just chose to because she, too, wanted to see him again.

"Come on." She stood, pulling him out of his seat. "Finish getting dressed. Then I'll drive you home."

"And tomorrow?" Gage drew her into his arms.

"You call me, and I invite you over for dinner."

"Count on it."

His kiss was demanding and possessive, verging on wild. Had Aubrey been wearing socks, they would have disappeared in a wisp of smoke. The spellbinding effects lasted only until they left the motor home.

As they walked hand in hand to the community center, Aubrey's tendency to expect trouble kicked in. She began to question her reasons for sleeping with Gage and inviting him over the following night—not because their farewell would be difficult and sad when she left, but after nearly three weeks of being with him on a steady basis, she might not want to leave Blue Ridge.

What, then, would become of the nursing career she loved?

Chapter Ten

Gage jerked back as a flame unexpectedly leapt up in front of his face, the heat from it stinging his skin.

"Hey, buddy," Marty said from beside him. "Watch it. You almost lost an eyebrow."

"You think I'd know better." Gage adjusted the controls on the front of their gas barbecue grill. The blue flame flickered once then promptly extinguished with a soft puff. Gage cursed under his breath. "The automatic ignition on this thing has never worked right."

"You guys ready for these?" Kelli came across the lawn toward them carrying a large platter heaped with hamburger patties.

"Not yet." Marty leaned over and gave his wife a peck on the check. "Gage can't get the grill lit."

"Firefighters." Kelli rolled her eyes and handed her husband the platter. "Here, let a layperson have at it."

Turning the knob ever so slowly, she depressed the ignition button twice in rapid succession. A small flame appeared, caught, then spread evenly beneath the artificial coals.

"Okay." Kelli straightened and swiped her hands together. "Give that a few minutes to warm up, and we're ready to rock and roll."

Gage looked first at her, then Marty. "Did she just whip my butt?"

"Hard," Marty said and broke into laughter.

"How'd you do that?" Gage asked. The temperamental grill had been giving the Raintree family grief for years.

Kelli waved her hand in the air. "Magic fingers, my friend."

Gage took out a scrubber and began to clean the grill. "Maybe after we eat you can show me your magic fingers again."

Marty put a possessive arm around Kelli's waist. "You got your own girl. Go play magic fingers with her and leave mine alone."

Yeah, thought Gage, he did have his own girl. At least for another two weeks.

"And speaking of girls…" Kelli sidled closer to Gage, who'd finished cleaning the grill and was now coating it with a nonstick spray. "I like Aubrey. A lot. I can't believe you two ever divorced."

"Kelli," Marty warned.

"I'm sorry." She gave an apologetic smile. "But you two are just so cute together."

"It's all right," Gage said, setting the can of spray down and picking up the hamburger patties. "I'm glad you like her."

When faced with the prospect of a rare Sunday afternoon off work, Gage had invited Marty and Kelli out to the ranch for a cookout. Now that he and Aubrey were officially dating, he wanted her to get to know his friends and for them to know her.

His mother, delighted with the prospect of entertaining Gage's captain, had outdone herself, whipping up her special recipe potato salad, pineapple coleslaw and corn on the cob to go with the hamburgers. Aubrey had brought two kinds of dessert. She and her grandmother were in the house helping his mother, along with Hannah. Gage's father, also in the mood to relax for once, was watching a ball game on TV.

"You going to ask her to stay in Blue Ridge with you?" Kelli smiled expectantly.

This time her husband's warning was accompanied by a stern scowl. "None of your business, sweetheart."

"I'm fond of Gage, I like seeing him happy. Aubrey makes him happy."

Gage couldn't agree more. Aubrey did indeed make him very happy.

The burgers sizzled as he set them on the grill. Kelli observed him with an eagle eye and when he was finished, went behind him with the spatula and rearranged all the hamburgers.

"I didn't know burgers cooked better in straight rows."

"That way the heat is more evenly distributed." She sighed impatiently. "Clearly you two only know how to put fires out, not cook with them."

"Is she this obsessive-compulsive at home?" Gage asked.

"Worse." Marty knocked back a swig of iced tea.

Both he and Gage would have preferred a cold beer but they made it a practice to avoid alcohol during fire season.

"Well, just so you know," Gage said, stepping aside so Kelli could more closely supervise the cooking hamburgers, "I'm not asking Aubrey to stay."

"Why?"

"Because she has her job to return to, for one." The conversation he and Aubrey had in the motor home last week came back to Gage in bits and pieces. "It's not fair of me to ask her to give it up." He didn't mention her freezing problem.

"I suppose you could commute and have a long-distance relationship." Kelli sprinkled seasoning on the hamburgers. "Vacations, holidays, three-day weekends."

Marty murmured, "Give it a rest," under his breath but she ignored him.

Gage tried to remember the last three-day weekend he'd had off and couldn't. Hell, he hadn't had a Sunday afternoon off in two months.

"I'm sure we'll work something out," he said with far more assurance than he felt.

Because of his promise not to pressure Aubrey, he hadn't brought up the subject of life after Blue Ridge with her.

Lately, however, as the days flew by, he'd begun to question his ability to hold out.

The back door opened, distracting Gage. Aubrey emerged with Hannah in tow, the two of them carrying plates and bowls and chatting a mile a minute. They headed for the table and chairs they'd set up earlier under the branches of a sprawling cottonwood tree.

She smiled at him from across the distance, and Gage felt a strong emotion tug at his heart. He wasn't just going to miss Aubrey when she left, he was going to be lost without her.

Again.

From inside the house, the phone rang. Gage could hear a distant echo of it coming from the barn. He told himself to relax. A ringing phone didn't automatically mean a fire. After all, his radio hadn't gone off and his cell phone remained silent.

But when his mother rushed through the back door, concern written all over her face, Gage knew this phone call wasn't social.

"Christine Peterson's on the line. Their haystack is on fire."

"Get a hold of the guys," Gage hollered to his mother. "Tell them I'll meet them at the station. And tell Mike to ready the engine."

In a small town the size of Blue Ridge, there was no dispatcher. Calls for the volunteer fire department came by telephone.

Before Gage could turn all the way around, Kelli took the spatula from his hands.

"Go," she said without preamble.

"I'll come with you." Marty jogged alongside Gage.

"You don't have to."

"This is a volunteer fire department, right? I'm volunteering."

Gage didn't refuse. They could always use the help. Hay fires could smoulder for days or turn nasty and burst into flames.

He spotted Aubrey on their race to his truck. "Come with us," he shouted. "In case there are any injuries."

She paused, uncertainty shadowing her features. It lasted only a second, long enough for Gage to wonder if he'd asked too much of her. In the next second she passed her stack of paper plates to Hannah and ran to join Gage and Marty at the truck.

The three of them piled into the cab and, without another word, tore out of the yard.

THEY COULD SEE the plume of white smoke for several miles before they arrived at the Petersons' place. Aubrey sat in the backseat of the engine, squished between Marty and Kenny Junior. Gage was up front with Mike, who drove, and Gus rode on the top. Aubrey hoped to God everything would be okay.

It had been over twenty minutes since the call had come in at the Raintree ranch. Fire could cause an amazing amount of damage in that time. And while it seemed to take forever, the Blue Ridge Volunteer Fire Department was the closest help. The *only* help. A house would burn to the ground long before an emergency vehicle from Pineville arrived.

Their wailing siren had drawn numerous onlookers. Adults spilled from their houses to watch the engine pass, and children waved at them from front yards. Two cars followed closely behind, to help, Aubrey hoped, not hinder.

The Petersons' place was in the middle of town on six acres. The possibility of the hay fire spreading to neighboring houses was slim, but the proximity of the Petersons' house and barn presented a danger. Burning embers carried on the breeze could easily ignite a roof, tree, or woodpile.

As the engine screamed toward the driveway, someone Aubrey didn't recognize pushed open a rolling gate. A half-dozen horses, evidently freed from their stalls in the barn, trotted around the front yard, bucking and kicking, and whinnying at all the commotion.

Mike drove the engine across the finely manicured lawn and past the small herd of horses to the barn in back of the house.

"Holy crap," Marty said when they got near the barn, his fingers poised on the door handle.

The reason for his expletive became quickly clear. The shade covering the haystack was in flames, the wooden posts and trusses holding the tin roof ablaze. Smoke poured from the haystack in a huge funnel, going up at least thirty feet before veering off at an angle.

John Peterson stood between the burning haystack and the barn, spraying water on the fire with a garden hose. He could have been spitting on it for all the good he did. A single garden hose was no match for this inferno.

Before the engine came to a complete stop, the guys were already piling out and donning the rest of their gear. Within the next minute, they had the hose unrolled and hooked up to the water tank on the engine. Kenny Junior turned a valve, and a blast of water a hundred times the size of the garden hose exploded from the nozzle.

"What can I do to help?" Aubrey asked. Since none of the Petersons appeared injured, her nursing skills weren't in demand.

"Unload the other hose from the back of the engine and unroll it," Gus told her. "We may need to pump water from the Millers' stock pond across the street if the tank runs dry."

"Okay." Aubrey glanced over her shoulder as she headed to the back of the engine. Gage held the nozzle, his feet planted solidly in place, and aimed it at the fire. Kenny Junior backed him up. The rest of the guys cleared the area around the fire, dragging, pushing, or driving anything and everything away.

"Jeremy, come back," Mrs. Peterson cried. She ran after a young boy—Aubrey assumed he was her grandson—who'd escaped the confines of the house.

The boy, no more than three, must have had aspirations to be a firefighter when he grew up. He refused to listen and kept running up the hill leading to the barn until he was alarmingly close to the fire.

"Get the hell out of here," his grandfather yelled. He'd gone over to the barn wall closest to the fire and was wetting it down with the hose.

Jeremy stopped in his tracks, evidently startled by his grandfather's brusque outburst, and began to cry.

"Come back," his grandmother called, huffing and puffing. She'd lost speed halfway up the hill, unable to catch her agile grandson.

Aubrey dropped the hose and bolted. She reached Jeremy and swooped him up in her arms.

"I've got you, sweetie pie."

Jeremy didn't want to be rescued. He wiggled and squirmed and hollered, "Snowflake," over and over in Aubrey's ear.

She was more than a little glad to present him safe and sound to his grandmother.

"Jeremy, honey, I told you to stay in the house. It's not safe out here."

Aubrey glanced back up the hill to the fire. The flames still raged despite being saturated with water. The four wooden posts holding the shade covering blazed like giant matchsticks.

Other than on TV, she'd never witnessed firefighters in action. A burning haystack might not compare to a city skyscraper in terms of danger, property damage and potential loss of life. But it was nonetheless terrifying, especially when Gage and his crew ventured close to the flames.

Beside Aubrey, Mrs. Peterson struggled to hold on to her rambunctious grandson. "He wants to find Snowflake."

"Is that one of the horses?"

"Heavens, no," Mrs. Peterson exclaimed. "She's our barn cat. A stray we recently took in. And wouldn't you know it, she produced a litter of kittens three weeks ago. In the haystack of all places."

Aubrey had been watching Gage fight the fire, only half listening to Mrs. Peterson. The older woman's last remark, however, had Aubrey paying rapt attention.

"The cat and kittens were in the haystack?" she gasped in horror, unable to consider the dire consequences.

"They got out. At least, we *think* they did. John saw Snowflake carrying one of the kittens into the barn right when we first noticed the smoke."

"One?" Aubrey asked. "How many did she have?"

"Four," Jeremy answered. He'd quit wiggling quite so much and hung on his grandmother's arm, attempting to move her. She stood steady as an iron post.

"He's been enthralled with the kittens," she explained. "Playing with them all week."

"Cats are very resourceful," Aubrey said. "And resilient. I'm sure Snowflake's fine." And at least *one* of her babies.

"Can't we go look for her, Grandma? Please?" Jeremy's whining intensified.

"No."

"But the kittens…"

Her voice softened. "We'll look for Snowflake the minute the fire's out. I promise."

"It is out." Though not fully extinguished, the firefighters' efforts had started to pay off. Already, the fire looked smaller in size and considerably less threatening.

"What do you think?" Mrs. Peterson asked Aubrey. "Is it safe to go into the barn?"

"The fire hasn't spread, and I don't think it will at this point."

Mrs. Peterson's glance alternated between her grandson and the barn. "I'll just take a quick walk through and see if I can spot Snowflake."

"Can I go with you?" Jeremy chirped.

"Absolutely not!" Aubrey and Mrs. Peterson said in unison. Jeremy frowned. "Not fair."

Aubrey reached out and rumpled his hair. "Maybe next time, kiddo, when you're a little older."

After returning Jeremy to the house, Mrs. Peterson went to the barn. Aubrey started up the hill, watching the firefighters. Gage and his crew had done their job. Smoke continued to pour from the blackened remains of the haystack but the fire was pretty much done for. The shade covering the haystack stood at an odd angle, the wooden columns now nothing but charred twigs.

If only there was something more she could do to help. Aubrey wasn't used to standing around in an emergency situation. Her adrenaline rush, which had kicked in back at the ranch when Gage asked her to accompany him and Marty, had yet to abate.

She was halfway to the engine when she heard a loud crash. She looked over and gave an involuntary shriek. One of the burnt columns had collapsed, and a piece of the tin roof the size of a door had fallen and hit the ground with a horrendous clatter just inches from where Gage stood.

He jumped back. So did Kenny Junior. They momentarily lost control of the hose.

Aubrey stared, transfixed, her heart lodged in her throat, her stomach twisted in knots. Had the piece of roof hit Gage, he would have been seriously injured. Possibly disfigured. Killed if it had landed on his head.

"We're all right," Gage hollered when Marty, Gus and Mike came running. He regained control of the hose, stepped back several feet and continued dousing the smouldering haystack.

And still Aubrey didn't move. She wanted to cry but no tears would come. It had happened again. In a moment of crisis, she'd frozen.

For how long she stared at Gage she didn't know. Seconds. Minutes.

"Man down!" Gus yelled.

Aubrey turned her head, though her feet remained anchored in place. Mr. Peterson sat on the ground, evidently dazed, his arms hanging loosely at his sides. Gus, who was working only a few feet away, reached Mr. Peterson first, then Mike. The two of them knelt down to talk to the older man.

Aubrey's legs at last responded, and she hurried to join them. "What's wrong?"

"Not sure yet," Gus responded.

"Mr. Peterson?" She also knelt, noting his pasty pallor and rapid breathing. She automatically reached for his wrist and took his pulse. It was uneven and accelerated.

"I'm okay. Just need to rest a minute." Sweat dotted his forehead.

He could be having a reaction to the roof collapsing or a touch of smoke inhalation but Aubrey suspected something more.

"Are you currently on any medications?"

"Yes."

"What kind?"

He listed his prescriptions. Aubrey recognized the names as those taken for a heart condition.

"You may have overdone it a bit." She eyed the fire. Gage still had the situation under control. They were safe where they were, for the moment anyway. "I want you to rest while I get something from the engine." She patted his arm. "I'll be right back."

Earlier, on the drive over, Aubrey had automatically taken a mental inventory of the available medical supplies and equipment and remembered seeing a portable oxygen tank.

She walked to the engine on shaky legs. Marty was there, unloading some shovels. At her request, he carried the oxygen tank to Mr. Peterson and helped her set it up. Mrs. Peterson arrived just as Aubrey was adjusting the valve.

"What happened?" she asked, her expression one of alarm.

Aubrey filled her in on the details.

"John! How many times have I told you to take it easy?"

"I'm all right," he grumbled.

"He probably is," Aubrey confirmed, "but I encourage you to call his doctor."

Mrs. Peterson fussed over her husband for several minutes.

Aubrey was relieved to see him grow stronger with each passing minute. They'd be able to move him into the house soon.

"Any sign of Snowflake?" she asked.

"Yes, thank goodness," Mrs. Peterson replied. "I found her and all four kittens in a bucket under the workbench."

"Jeremy will be glad to hear it."

Aubrey had been crouched beside Mr. Peterson and shifted so she could see the fire. Mike had taken over the hose with Marty backing him up. For all intents and purposes, the fire was out, though it continued to smoulder and hiss.

Gage came toward them, rolling his shoulders to relieve tension, a tired smile on his face.

"How's our patient doing?"

Aubrey couldn't help thinking if the piece of tin roof had fallen just a few inches more to the right, Gage might be the patient in her care along with Mr. Peterson.

"Better," she said, fighting to keep her voice steady.

"You really should consider becoming a volunteer medic for the Hotshots." Gage gazed down at her, his eyes filled with affection and admiration. "You're a natural at this."

But Aubrey didn't feel like a natural. Far, far from it.

Chapter Eleven

Gage clipped his radio to his belt and walked into the kitchen. His mother stood at the counter, wrapping four large chocolate chip cookies in plastic. She dropped them in the ice chest he'd left on the counter.

"Hey." He came up behind her and gave her an affectionate squeeze. "That's my job."

"I baked these this afternoon. Thought you might like them for your picnic."

"Thanks, Mom."

Gage had invited Aubrey on an evening picnic and told her he'd bring the food. Not much of a cook, he'd made arrangements with Harold Sage, the owner of Sage's Bar and Grill. Some of the stuff Harold fixed seemed a bit strange, but he promised Gage that Aubrey would be delighted at the gourmet fare.

"I can't believe she's leaving next Friday," his mom said. "It seems like she just arrived."

Removing a bottle of chilled wine from the refrigerator, Gage placed it in the cooler, the perpetual lead weight in his stomach growing heavier. He hadn't been able to stop thinking of Aubrey's imminent departure for days now.

They'd spent every free minute together since that day in the motor home two and a half weeks ago—which, because of their hectic schedules, wasn't nearly enough. Gage had been gone for four of those days working a fire in Utah. Because his departure coincided with semester break at summer school, his sister was able to pick up most of the slack at the ranch.

Right after the fire at the Petersons', she gave in to Dr. Ferguson's persistent needling and agreed to volunteer at the clinic every other afternoon. News spread fast and before long, she had more patients than she could handle.

He hadn't yet been able to convince her to volunteer with the Hotshots. Her personal demons continued to haunt her and Gage wished there was more he could do for her than lend the occasional ear.

For his part, he sailed along on a tide of contentment. He and Aubrey took long walks, went horseback riding, had dinner and then went dancing at a honky-tonk in Pineville, and generally hung out together.

They'd also had sex. Lots of it, frequenting the motor home whenever possible. One night, they tossed a sleeping bag and pillows in the bed of his truck and went on a drive to Signal Point. Gage would always remember the sight of Aubrey, naked and sitting astride him, moonlight glinting off her auburn hair as she bent down to kiss him.

He'd be lying if he said he didn't want their picnic tonight to end much the same.

"Look, honey." His mom took a sip of her iced tea as if to fortify herself. "It's none of my business, but I'm asking anyway. What's going to happen with you and Aubrey when she leaves? Have you two discussed it?"

"We have. Though not recently." Difficult as it was for him, he'd kept his word and not pressured Aubrey into any kind of commitment. "She's leaving, and I'm staying. For now," he added on impulse and then wondered why he did.

"Does that mean she's coming back in the near future? Or are you moving to Tucson?"

"How would you feel if I did?"

His mom considered before answering, rubbing the condensation forming on the outside of her glass with her thumb.

"Ranching's a funny thing. It's either in your blood or not. You might look like your father, but you take after me in a lot of respects. I married into the lifestyle and accepted it because I love your father. I refuse to impose that same lifestyle on my children if it's not what they truly and honestly want. Hannah does, I think. You, on the other hand, have fought to get away from ranching since you were a kid."

"For all the good it's done me."

"You're an adult now. No one can stop you from leaving, including your father." Susan smiled ruefully. "Though he probably thinks he can."

Gage shut the lid on the ice chest. "I can't leave the ranch. Not while Hannah's in college."

"Granted, you being gone would make things harder, but not impossible."

"We wouldn't be having this conversation if Dad weren't ashamed to ask people for help. That's the real reason he wants me to stay. All that talk about family responsibility and obligation is just so he can save face."

"Don't be so hard on him, sweetheart. Growing older is rough, more so on some of us than others."

"It doesn't have to be. We live in a town where nine-tenths of the population would bend over backward to help a friend and neighbor. Insisting I stay is selfish and unfair."

"He has his pride," Susan said, her tone sharp.

Gage realized he'd gone too far and made an effort to control his temper. "No one would think less of him if he asked for an occasional hand."

"Of course they wouldn't. But he doesn't see it that way. His gout has done as much emotional damage as physical."

What would it be like to live with reoccurring and debilitating pain? Gage tried to imagine. Like his father, he'd probably resent having to slow down and rely on others. But he doubted he'd force his family to give up their goals and ambitions in order to compensate for his loss of abilities.

Susan went back to rinsing dishes and stacking them in the dishwasher. "If you want to leave with Aubrey next week, do it. We'll manage one way or another."

"How?"

It was probably just as well Gage's dad had ridden over to the Double S Ranch on the other side of Neglian Creek and wasn't home to hear their conversation.

"I'll quit my job," Susan answered.

"You love working at the real estate office."

"I can always go back to work when Hannah graduates college."

"Forget it."

His mom was attempting to compromise, and while he appreciated the effort, he'd have none of it. She'd already made enough sacrifices for the sake of their family. Gage wouldn't be the reason behind another one. Nor would he put his family in worse financial straits. They needed his mom's income.

"What about Kenny Junior?" she asked. "He might be willing to work part-time in exchange for room and board."

Gage's mental wheels began to spin. "Maybe."

"We could fix up the old bunkhouse," Susan went on to say. "All it really needs is a good cleaning, a fresh coat of paint and a couple minor repairs. Kenny Junior's not fussy."

"I'll talk to him," Gage said, liking the arrangement more and more by the second.

"And I'll talk to your dad. But I need to approach him just right." Susan folded the dish towel she'd been using, hung it over the oven handle to dry and faced Gage. "Put it to him like we're doing Kenny Junior a favor and not the other way around."

The lead weight in Gage's stomach felt suddenly lighter. Was it possible? Could he leave with Aubrey next week and move with her to Tucson? Excitement grabbed hold of him as his mind soared in a dozen different directions.

He'd have to put in his notice with the Blue Ridge

Hotshots. Hopefully they'd give him a good recommendation, as Gage had no intentions of quitting firefighting anytime soon. The Tucson Hotshots were a top-notch outfit and if they weren't hiring, he'd look elsewhere. With a little grooming, Kenny Junior could take over as head of the Blue Ridge Volunteer Fire Department.

All at once his mind ground to a screeching halt.

What about Aubrey?

Gage realized he'd been making one very large assumption. His and Aubrey's agreement to date was only for the duration of her stay in Blue Ridge. She might not welcome him tagging along with her to Tucson, moving into her apartment with her. Just because the last couple of weeks had been unbelievably great for him didn't mean they were great for her, too.

But, oh, they *had* been great weeks. Better than their marriage. Gage and Aubrey hadn't argued once. Come to think of it, they'd never argued before they were married, either. Did their problems start only when they were cohabitating?

He'd talk with Aubrey tonight, he decided. Try and get an inkling of how she felt about him—*them*—before springing any plans on her.

"Your dad will dig in his heels at the beginning," Susan continued. "He won't like it that you're leaving."

"Dig in his heels?" Gage had to laugh. "He'll blow his stack. And make everyone's life miserable."

"Only because he'll miss you." His mom went to Gage and gave him a hug. "And so will I. Terribly."

"I'll miss you, too."

"Tucson isn't so far. You can come up for a visit every few months." She stepped back, and her eyes glistened with tears. "I've always loved Aubrey. She's a very special person. Nothing would make me happier than to see you two married again."

"Wait just a second." Gage put out a hand. "Who said anything about marriage?"

"Well, I…"

"Let's take this one step at a time. I have to talk to Aubrey first."

Not that Gage wasn't in favor of walking down the aisle with Aubrey again. He just didn't want to rush things. Too much too soon was what had landed them in trouble the first time.

"She loves you. It's obvious."

Did she?

Susan's smile spoke volumes. "And I think the feeling's mutual."

Was it?

He lifted the ice chest off the counter. "I'd better load up the truck and head out of here. I told Aubrey I'd pick her up at six-thirty."

His cell phone abruptly rang, and Gage clenched his jaw. He didn't want anything to interrupt his plans with Aubrey tonight. Setting the ice chest back down, he checked the caller ID before answering. His pulse jumped when he recognized the number.

"Raintree."

"Gage. It's Larry Newcombe."

"Yes, sir."

"Sorry to bother you so late in the day. We were in meetings all afternoon, and we just now got out."

"That's quite all right." Gage told himself not to leap to conclusions, but it was hard not to. There were only a handful of reasons why a commanding officer called a Hotshot and it wasn't to report for duty.

"I didn't think you'd mind. Not when you heard what I had to say. Congratulations, son. Your promotion to crew leader came through."

Excitement and elation surged through Gage. It was a minor miracle he was able to maintain a level voice. "Thank you, sir." He looked over at his mother and grinned from ear to ear.

Her expression changed from curiosity to happiness, and she mouthed, "Did you get the promotion?"

He nodded, simultaneously listening to Commander Newcombe outline the responsibilities of his new position, which he pretty much knew thanks to Marty.

"Be proud of yourself," Commander Newcombe finished up. "There were a lot of qualified candidates to choose from, and we picked you."

"I'm very proud. And thank you again, sir."

After Gage disconnected, he gave his mother a bear hug, kissed her soundly on the cheek and swung her around the kitchen.

"Stop it," she squealed, laughing all the while.

Gage swung her around once more for good measure. Damn, but he felt good. He'd been waiting a long time for this promotion and had worked hard for it.

"I'm so happy for you, sweetheart," Susan said once she caught her breath.

"That makes two of us."

"I know Aubrey will be happy, too."

Gage's grin went slack. Not ten minutes ago he'd been seriously contemplating returning with her to Tucson. Then his promotion had come through.

His mother must have sensed the direction of his thoughts for she asked, "What are you going to do? Stay or go?"

"I don't know." He hefted the ice chest onto his hip. "Guess I'll talk to Aubrey tonight."

And say what?

Did it really matter?

She'd made it clear from the start her return to Blue Ridge was temporary. Which meant he either stayed here, or declined his promotion, let one of those other qualified candidates have it and went to Tucson with Aubrey.

Hell of a choice.

Just as he reached the back door, Biscuit began barking. "Are you expecting anyone?" he asked.

"No." His mother followed him out onto the back porch. Biscuit stood at full attention near the edge of the yard, lifting her head every few seconds to sound another alarm. Not a vehicle was in sight.

"That's funny," Susan mused aloud.

Gage heard it then, the loud clatter of galloping hoofbeats. As he and his mother stared, his father's big buckskin gelding came charging up the side road for all he was worth, reins flapping and stirrups bouncing. Panic shot through Gage.

Where was his dad?

He dropped the ice chest and ran. The exhausted animal had reached the gate and stood there, sides heaving and nostrils flaring. Shoving open the gate, Gage gathered the reins and gave the horse a quick once-over, but there were no clues as to his father's whereabouts.

His mother came rushing toward him. She'd evidently gone back into the house because in her hand she held a walkie-talkie. As she approached, he could hear her frantic attempts to raise his father.

"Joseph, are you there? Can you hear me? Come in."

Her only reply was empty air.

Stopping in her tracks, she gazed at Gage, clearly on the verge of tears.

"Don't worry, Mom. I'll find him." He took the walkie-talkie from her and pressed the reins into her hands. "You unsaddle Comanche while I bring the ATV around. Call over to the Double S Ranch when you're done. See if one of their guys can drive the road to Neglian Creek crossing. I'll take the west trail and meet up with him there. One of us will find Dad."

"What if you don't?"

"Then we call the sheriff."

"Maybe we shouldn't wait."

Gage glanced at the sun dipping low toward the distant mountains. Not much daylight remained. "Put a call into the volunteer fire department, too." He bent and kissed her cheek. "Dad's going to be mad as hell at us for having half the county out looking for him."

His mom's breath hitched. "I'll take my chances."

Ten minutes later Gage crested the rise a half mile from their house. While the ATV idled, he had a look around. The trail to Neglian Creek was more than a path but less than a road, too narrow for a full-sized vehicle. Some spots were wide open, others thick with clusters of trees and brush.

His dad could be anywhere. Walking along the shaded creek bank. Resting on a fallen log. Lying hurt somewhere, unconscious from a fall.

Guilt ate a gigantic hole in Gage's middle. His dad really was in no shape to run the ranch alone. But then, maybe he didn't have to. With Gage's promotion coming through, him leaving with Aubrey had been reduced from a distinct possibility to a mere option.

It wasn't until he revved the engine that he remembered his date with her. Pulling the walkie-talkie from his pocket, he depressed the button on the side and raised his mother almost immediately.

"Do me a favor, Mom. Call Aubrey and postpone our date."

"All right." She updated him on her conversation with the Double S Ranch then signed off so she could call the sheriff.

Gage hit the gas and flew down the slope, dust and pebbles shooting out from behind the ATV. If they didn't find his dad soon, chances were they'd have to call off the search until morning.

A lot could happen to a person alone in the hills and on foot during the hours between nightfall and sunrise. Gage slowed to take a sharp turn and tried not to dwell on the many grave possibilities.

AUBREY CLICKED the "submit order" icon on her laptop computer screen. A second later, a confirmation page appeared. She reviewed the list of items carefully. Satisfied everything was there, she clicked on the "proceed to payment" icon.

"Here you are." Grandma Rose teetered into the kitchen, a cane in each hand. She'd been doing well with her rehabilitation but still suffered periodic bouts of unsteadiness. "What are you up to?"

"I just finished placing your first grocery order." Aubrey sat at the table, her laptop hooked up to the kitchen phone. "It'll arrive in three days."

"I don't like the idea of buying my groceries with a computer," Grandma Rose complained. She eyed the laptop as if it were an alien contraption. "I enjoy picking out my food."

"I know. And you'll be able to do your own shopping when Mrs. Payne or someone else takes you into Pineville with them on their errands. This is for times they can't. If you run out of something before the regular order is scheduled, call me and I can take care of it from any computer no matter where I am."

Grandma Rose's grumble had a resigned tone to it. She pulled out the chair next to Aubrey and sat down, struggling slightly with her canes. Aubrey resisted the urge to jump up and help. Her grandmother had to learn to do things by herself if she was going to live independently.

"I've also ordered you a Guardian Angel. It's supposed to arrive tomorrow by overnight mail."

"What's a Guardian Angel?"

"It's a small device you wear around your neck. If you fall or need help for any reason, you push a button. It automatically transmits a signal to Mrs. Payne, the emergency dispatcher in Pineville and the Blue Ridge Volunteer Fire Department."

"Sounds like a lot of fuss to me."

"I really hope you'll wear it. If not for yourself, for Mom. She worries about you being alone."

More importantly, should anything happen, Gage or one of his crew would arrive at the house in a matter of minutes. Aubrey took considerable comfort knowing he'd be there for her grandmother in the weeks and months to come.

Unlike her.

Aubrey put thoughts of leaving from her mind, something

she'd been doing with increasing frequency of late. Gage was due to arrive any minute, and they were going on an evening picnic. She didn't know where, he'd made all the arrangements and refused to impart any specifics when she'd asked.

She really wanted the date to go well. They had so little time left together. True to his promise, he'd not once asked her to stay, but she felt pretty confident the thought had occurred to him. It had certainly occurred to her. Often. How could it not? She cared for Gage and their recent time together had been wonderful. It didn't take much effort for her to picture herself living on the Raintree ranch with him again—though not in the motor home—and volunteering at the clinic.

Would that be enough to keep her happy? More than anything, Aubrey missed her job. Part of her dreaded returning, afraid she hadn't conquered her crisis in confidence. The larger part of her, however, couldn't wait to walk into the hospital and experience that familiar rush of adrenaline coursing through her veins.

Dispensing antibiotics and taking blood pressure readings at the clinic, while enjoyable, couldn't compare to a busy E.R.

"Shouldn't Gage be here by now?" Grandma Rose squinted at the clock on the wall.

"He's running a little late, I guess." Aubrey unplugged the phone line from her computer. Selfishly, she hoped he hadn't been called to a fire. "You'll be all right while I'm gone?"

Grandma Rose dismissed Aubrey's concerns with a snort.

"Call me on my cell phone if you need anything." When her grandmother didn't answer, Aubrey touched her arm. "You okay?"

Grandma Rose sniffled and rubbed her nose. "Silly, I suppose. It's just that I've gotten kind of used to your bossiness. Going to miss it. Going to miss you, too."

"I'll be back. First long weekend I have off work."

"How does Gage feel about you leaving?"

Aubrey tensed. She wasn't ready to discuss her and Gage's

future relationship or potential lack of it. A classic case of avoidance, without question. Recognizing a behavior pattern, however, didn't change it.

Fortunately, a ringing in another part of the house relieved her of answering the question. She went over to the counter and plugged in the phone she'd unplugged for her computer.

"Hello."

"Aubrey? Is that you?"

"Susan?"

"Yes. Thank goodness I reached you. The line's been busy for ages."

"What's wrong?" Aubrey frowned. Her former mother-in-law sounded upset.

"Gage asked me to call. He's going to have to postpone your date."

Her shoulders slumped. She'd been afraid of this. "A fire?"

"No. Joseph's missing. Gage went looking for him."

"Oh, my gosh!" Aubrey instantly straightened and glanced at her grandmother, who was watching her with concerned interest. "What happened?"

"We don't know for sure," Susan said. "He was feeling good today and rode over to the Double S Ranch to talk with the owner about sharing some water rights. Then an hour ago, his horse came home without him. I've called the sheriff. They sent a couple men out but don't think there's much they can do until morning. Gage and the foreman from the Double S are driving the trails to Neglian Creek crossing looking for Joseph."

Aubrey's heart went out to Susan. "Would you like me to come over and stay with you?"

Susan's voice cracked with emotion. "You wouldn't mind?"

"Of course not."

"I've been trying to reach Hannah. She's out with some friends tonight and not picking up her cell phone."

"I'll be right there."

Aubrey quickly filled her grandmother in on the situation

with Joseph and then left for the Raintree Ranch. When no one answered her knock on the front door, she went inside.

She found Susan in the kitchen, sitting on the floor with her back against the refrigerator, a walkie-talkie in her hand, and sobbing as if her world were falling apart.

Chapter Twelve

"Mom! Come in, Mom!" Gage tossed the walkie-talkie on the seat of the borrowed Jeep and stomped on the gas. "She's crying and won't answer." He shot his passenger an exasperated scowl before turning his attention back to the road.

"Your mother always did have an emotional streak a mile wide."

"Goddamn it, Dad. She loves you."

Joseph swore far more colorfully than his son when they hit a pothole, and he came six inches off the seat. "Take it easy, will you? I'm not made of stone."

Gage slowed, but only because his mother would never forgive him if he didn't deliver his father in one piece.

"Hello. Gage, are you there?" A scratchy version of Aubrey's voice floated up from the seat beside him.

He grabbed the walkie-talkie and put it to his mouth. "Aubrey? Is that you?"

"Yes. I'm here with your mother."

Gage's anger and frustration instantly lessened. Aubrey was there. Waiting for him. "Glad to hear it."

"How's your father?"

"A bit bruised, but ornery as ever. We should be home in a few minutes."

"See you then. Oh, wait! We can meet you at the clinic if your dad needs medical attention."

Joseph leaned sideways and spoke into the walkie-talkie. "The only thing I need is a hot shower and a couple of aspirin." He then glowered at Gage. "No way is your ex-wife examining me. You understand?"

"She's a nurse, Dad."

"I don't care if she was the only medical help for five hundred miles and I was bleeding to death. She'd not examining me."

Gage shook his head, amazed yet again at the depths of his father's stubborn and utterly useless pride. "Why didn't you call in? Could have saved Mom a whole lot of grief and the rest of us a whole lot of bother."

"I figured on making it back to the Double S."

"Five miles on *your* ankle? I don't think so."

"I could've done it."

"And been laid up for weeks afterward. Have you no consideration whatsoever for the rest of us?"

"That's enough out of you," Joseph snapped.

Gage shut up only because arguing with his father was an exercise in futility.

Joseph had been anything but a fountain of knowledge since being picked up. Nonetheless, Gage had been able to piece together most of what happened thanks to the Double S foreman.

His father, upon reaching Neglian Creek crossing, decided a short break was in order and dismounted. Comanche evidently spooked at who knew what and bolted, leaving Joseph stranded. Given Comanche's placid disposition and proven dependability, Gage suspected there was more to the story. If so, his father wasn't telling.

With the Double S Ranch being half as far as the Raintree Ranch, Joseph opted to head back the way he'd come. The Double S foreman found him on the road and contacted Gage. They met up at a halfway point between the neighboring ranches. The foreman generously offered Gage the use of his Jeep and took the ATV, agreeing to swap vehicles sometime tomorrow.

No big deal.

And yet it had been a big deal, all because his father had refused to report in.

Why?

Gage pulled to a stop in front of the main gate and shoved the Jeep into Park. "Your ankle gave out, didn't it?"

"What are you talking about?" Joseph made no effort to get out and open the gate.

"Your ankle gave out while you were mounting Comanche and you fell. Or maybe you got bucked off and landed face-first in the creek."

Several seconds passed. Finally, Joseph leaned his head back and stared at the darkening sky.

"I wouldn't mind so much if it had been my face." He grimaced and gingerly rubbed his backside. "Get me home, will you, and out of this dad-gum torture contraption."

Gage was tempted to laugh at the ironic justice fate had seen fit to dispense. The flash of genuine pain in his father's expression stopped him.

"What if I weren't here to bail you out? What would you have done then?" As soon as the words left his mouth, he realized he was asking himself the questions and not just his father.

"If you quit firefighting, it wouldn't be a problem," Joseph grumbled.

"I meant not here in Blue Ridge."

"Gone?" His father's brow knitted in confusion. "Since when?" Understanding apparently dawned on him as he let out a grunt. "It's Aubrey. You're thinking of going with her to Tucson."

"Before we get into another argument, let me clarify something. I'm only considering going with her."

"You can't leave the ranch," Joseph said firmly.

"The hell I can't." Gage hit the steering wheel with his fist. "I'm thirty years old, Dad. I'll do whatever I damn well please." His voice rose. "Leave Blue Ridge or stay. Be a firefighter or not."

His father stared at him, not with anger or hostility but amusement.

"Whàt?" Gage barked.

Joseph leaned his head back and chuckled.

"Glad one of us finds the situation funny," Gage said.

"It's just for a minute there, you sounded a lot like me."

Gage frowned. He'd thought the same thing the other day and hadn't liked it.

"I remember telling my father off," Joseph said, his tone reflective. "He didn't much cotton to my choices, either."

"You always wanted to go into ranching."

"True."

"So what choice could you have possibly made he didn't like?"

"I married your mother."

Gage's jaw went momentarily slack.

"She wasn't from Blue Ridge," Joseph went on. "And she wasn't from a ranching family. Your grandpa was dead certain she'd corrupt me. Lure me away from the ranch."

"What are you talking about? Grandpa adored Mom."

"Eventually. But not at first."

"Aubrey's not going to lure me away, Dad."

"I don't suppose she is. How could she? Firefighting did that a long time ago."

"No, it didn't." Gage came to a stop at the intersection leading to town and stared his father straight in the face. "It's probably the only thing that's kept me in Blue Ridge these past years."

Joseph returned Gage's stare. "I think I'm only just now starting to realize that."

"Let's go." Gage extended his hand to Aubrey and pulled her to her feet.

"Where?"

"On our picnic."

"You sure?"

They'd been sitting on the family room couch, watching

a sitcom neither of them found funny, and waiting for Gage's mother to finish tending to his father. Aubrey had assumed their date was cancelled, so Gage's sudden announcement caught her off guard.

"Yeah, I'm sure. Dad insists he's fine, Mom doesn't need us and Hannah's on her way home. No reason we can't stick to the original plan."

Considering the tense mood both Gage and his dad were in, vacating the house for a couple of hours seemed like a good idea.

"Okay. Let's go." Aubrey grabbed her purse and shut off the TV while Gage went to inform his parents of their plans.

It soon became apparent where Gage was taking her. Bouncing down the dirt road in his truck, Aubrey had to grin. His choice of a picnic location was perfect and, she supposed, fitting. Ten minutes later they parked and climbed out.

The zigzagging beam of Gage's flashlight guided them through the darkness and along the slippery, winding trail. Low-hanging tree limbs blocked their path and required periodic swatting, as did a hungry mosquito or two. The potent smell of damp earth invaded Aubrey's nostrils, triggering a wave of nostalgia. The gurgle of rushing creek water combined with the chirp and buzz of nocturnal animal life inspired still more memories.

Their secret spot.

Why, she wondered, had Gage brought her here? To remember? Or did he hope to create new memories, ones to see them through the coming separation?

"Wait a sec." Gage bent down, swept aside a curtain of dangling willow tree branches and disappeared inside the secluded shelter. Placing the ice chest on a semi-level patch of ground, he stuck a hand out to her. "Pass me the sleeping bag and pillows."

She did, then parted the branches and joined him.

Their secret spot had lost none of its magic. Seeing moonlight shimmering off the water's glassy surface through a veil of leafy willow tree branches elicited a wistful sigh from Aubrey.

"Nice, huh?" Gage asked.

"*Very* nice."

The temperature inside the shelter was several degrees cooler than outside and felt good on her bare arms as they arranged their small camp to their liking.

Sitting beside her on the sleeping bag, Gage opened the ice chest and rummaged around inside. He removed two long-stemmed wineglasses and a bottle of Chardonnay, pouring them each a generous portion. Before taking a sip, Gage lifted his glass to Aubrey's cheek and rubbed the rim along her jawline.

"Here's to you," he murmured.

The sensation of smooth, chilled glass against her skin sent silken ribbons of pleasure spiraling through her.

They clinked glasses, shared a lingering stare ripe with promise, then sipped the tart, heady wine. While Aubrey lit three stubby candles and set them on a broad, flat rock, Gage served the food, which was nothing like Aubrey expected.

"Pâté and toast triangles?"

"You don't like pâté?" Gage's expression was crestfallen.

"No, I love it." She couldn't stop the laugh bubbling up from her throat. "I just didn't think you did."

He relaxed and resumed removing sealed plastic storage containers from the ice chest and spreading them out on the sleeping bag. "I've never tried it."

"What if you hate the taste?"

"There aren't many foods I can't choke down."

Having witnessed his ravenous hunger on multiple occasions, Aubrey couldn't agree more.

The next half hour flew by with Gage and Aubrey enjoying a veritable smorgasbord of delicacies—everything from miniature roasted potatoes to mango and kiwi salad to pickled herring.

"Now, this I like." Gage took another bite of baklava and chewed contentedly.

"It's Greek," Aubrey said, licking remnants of the sinfully rich pastry from her fingers.

"Let me do that."

He snatched her hand in midair and, before she could stop him, began nibbling.

"Quit it." She giggled and squirmed and then went utterly limp when his tongue probed her sensitive fingertips.

"Don't ever let anyone tell you that fingers aren't an erogenous zone," he murmured between licks.

Above the swaying treetops, a zillion and one stars twinkled in a blue-black velvet sky. Aubrey laid her head on Gage's lap, taking in the magnificent view. "Did you know the human body has something like a hundred erogenous zones?"

"You don't say?"

"It's true."

"I not only believe you, I'm willing to test each and every one of them." He lowered his head to her ear and gently tugged on the lobe with his teeth.

Her heart gave a small—make that a large—pitter-patter. "You're impossible."

His lips were sticky with honey from the baklava and incredibly delicious. They were also remarkably proficient in shutting her up when molded firmly to her own lips.

Drunk on desire more than wine, she curled an arm around his neck. Pulling him closer, she took control of the kiss despite her lower position. Her advantage didn't last long. Gage slipped out from under her and in a swift move Casanova would admire, pinned her beneath him on the sleeping bag.

What remained of their picnic dinner was instantly forgotten.

He nuzzled the fine hair at her temple. "Tell me. Is this one of your hundred erogenous zones?"

"Mmm. Maybe."

"And this?" He nudged her head back and pressed his mouth to the side of her throat where her pulse beat.

"How'd you guess?"

His hand breached the hem of her T-shirt and snuck up her rib cage.

"What about—"

"Enough talk." She silenced him with a provocative kiss calculated to tease and entice.

Gage evidently agreed. Finding far more interesting things to do with his mouth than converse, he said nothing more for several incredibly sensual minutes while he removed her clothes. Wherever his hands touched her body, his mouth followed. She watched unabashedly as he drew a nipple into his mouth, licking and suckling the taut tip. She continued watching, even when he moved lower. Small sounds of delight escaped when his tongue dipped into her belly button.

"When's it my turn?" she asked after yet another breathless shudder.

"Not yet."

Gage parted her thighs, cupped her bottom and lifted her hips. Aubrey waited in torturous, glorious anticipation. He took too damn long, tracing moist circles with his tongue on the insides of her thighs rather than concentrating on the areas that would do the most good. When his mouth finally found her center, she nearly cried out. Within minutes, he had her in a state of near frenzy. She might have teetered on the edge a bit longer but his tongue probed deeper, found her most responsive erogenous zone yet, and sent her flying skyward to float among the zillion and one stars.

Upon her return to Earth, she found Gage hovering over her. "That was a pretty neat trick," she said.

"You liked it?" His smile smacked of sheepishness.

"Mmm." She wriggled beneath him and reached for the zipper of his jeans. "Can I try?"

"Fair's fair, I suppose."

Once he lay naked beside her, she took his full and heavy arousal into her hands and then into her mouth. If the ragged groans emanating from his chest were any indication, she then took him on one incredible ride.

"Come here." He tugged on her arm, pulling her on top of him.

"I wasn't finished," she complained, though not seriously.

"Trust me, you're hardly finished."

He pulled a condom from what appeared to be thin air. She discovered one or two more of his erogenous zones while he covered himself, distracting him as much as possible. When he finished, she straddled his hips and guided him inside her.

"This is better," she crooned, rocking back and forth in a seductive rhythm.

"Not quite."

"No?"

He framed her face with his hands and gathered her to him. When their lips were within kissing distance, Aubrey unfurled her legs and stretched out.

"Now, this is what I had in mind." Gage wrapped his arms around her and anchored her to him.

Every inch of her body from breast to toe melded to every inch of his, leaving only enough space remaining for a few molecules of air.

He moved slowly, withdrawing from her and then plunging back inside, quickly bringing Aubrey to the verge of another shattering climax. She'd never felt so close to Gage. So joined in every way. Physically, emotionally, and spiritually.

"Eyes," he said, his voice ragged, "are an erogenous zone, too."

"How so?" she managed in a strained whisper. He was so hard, so very deep inside her. Aubrey gasped and bucked slightly.

"Watching yours while I make you climax is a giant turn-on for me."

His words reached her through a sensual haze as she gave herself over to an array of exquisite sensations.

"Open your eyes, sweetheart. Look at me."

She did and knew exactly what he'd been talking about.

His dark eyes, staring hotly into hers, were incredibly arousing. Aubrey quit fighting and promptly lost it. Again.

Gage followed by a few seconds. Her limbs like liquid, she rolled off him, utterly exhausted and, at the same time, deliriously content. Hands clasped, they stared at the leafy ceiling of their shelter, rewarding themselves with a well-earned rest.

She couldn't help but recall their last visit to this place. Gage had lain beside her as he did now and asked her to marry him. Aubrey certainly didn't expect history to repeat itself, yet she suffered a tiny pang of disappointment when the moment passed without him proposing.

Loathe to separate, they snuggled and chatted about nothing in particular. Eventually, the moon sank beneath the far-off mountain peaks and the temperature dropped several degrees, turning the pleasantly cool air to downright chilly. Two of the candles had burned out, leaving hard wax puddles on the rock. By the light of the remaining candle they dressed and packed the ice chest. Content to stroll arm in arm, they said little on the return walk to Gage's truck.

Halfway home, Gage broke the silence.

"I got some good news earlier today."

"You did?" She smiled in expectation. "What?"

"I've been promoted to crew leader."

"That's wonderful! Why didn't you say something when you were opening the wine? We could have made a toast."

"Stay in Blue Ridge." Gage found her hand on the truck seat and brought it to his lap. "Live with me. Don't go back to Tucson."

"Wow." Aubrey hadn't seen that coming. Then again, wasn't she hoping for a similar declaration not forty-five minutes earlier?

"Damn." He grimaced. "That didn't come out right. But I'm not sorry I asked."

"We talked about this already." She chose her words carefully. The last thing she wanted was to end their truly lovely evening with an argument.

"There's no rule saying we can't talk about it again." He didn't look at her. The single-lane, tree-lined road was pitch-black and required his total concentration. "We deserve more time together, a chance to see where our relationship is going."

"I need to return to my job. I explained all that to you and thought you understood."

"You'd only have to give up your job until Hannah graduates." A hairpin turn loomed ahead. Gage swung the truck hard to the right. Ghostly limbs of overgrown pine trees slapped the passenger door causing Aubrey to flinch. "After that, I'd move to Tucson," Gage said when they exited the turn.

"You'd move?"

"Actually, I talked to Mom about it this afternoon. We were thinking Kenny Junior might be willing to work on the ranch in exchange for room and board."

"Really?"

It surprised Aubrey to learn that Gage would willingly leave his family and home so they could be together. Surprised *and* pleased.

"Your dad's gout will probably worsen over time, not improve. You sure you'd feel comfortable leaving, even after Hannah graduates?"

"She can handle the ranch, no problem. And besides, Dad listens to her more than he does Mom and me. If Kenny Junior's there, so much the better."

"What about my father?" Aubrey asked.

"What about him?"

"You and he aren't exactly buddies."

"We get along fine."

"You've seen him once in the last ten years. At my grandfather's funeral. And you spoke to each other only when necessary."

"So he and I aren't the best of pals. It's you I'd be living with, not him."

And wouldn't her father be tickled pink about that arrangement? She decided to lay that obstacle to rest and tackle another.

"If I were to stay in Blue Ridge and move in with you, and that's a big if, where would we live?"

"On the ranch."

"Not in the motor home. Please."

"God, no." He laughed. "We'd fix up the old bunkhouse. Later on, after we left for Tucson, Kenny Junior could move in if he was so inclined."

The notion of residing on the Raintree ranch did appeal to Aubrey. She'd loved that aspect of her and Gage's brief marriage. Still, it wasn't that simple. Country life was and had always been a summer vacation for her. A temporary break from the mad rush of the city. Could she survive peace and quiet on a long-term basis?

"What about income? Your family can't afford to feed and clothe another person, not one who isn't earning their keep. And let's face it, I'm no cowhand."

"I bet the town would hire you on at the clinic, part-time at least. The folks here are crazy about you. Just look at how many patients swarm the place on the days you work."

"I do enjoy working at the clinic." And on the plus side, she'd be nearby should her grandmother require anything. "But I miss my job. You and I are a lot alike when it comes to work, you know. We're both adrenaline junkies. You get your fix from fighting fires, I get mine from the E.R."

"Maybe there's something else you can do to take the place of the E.R."

"Like what?"

"Go back to college."

"College?"

"Why not?"

"I didn't realize Pineville College had a master's program for nursing."

Gage paid her sarcasm no mind. "They probably don't. Of course, you *could* change your studies to ranching."

"Ah…right."

Houses came into view as they reached the outskirts of town. Cutter's Market had four parked cars out front, evidence they were doing a booming late-night business by Blue Ridge standards.

"I'm only trying to explore some possibilities," he snapped.

"Which is good." Aubrey leaned over and kissed Gage's cheek. He was trying to compromise, and she was resisting his every suggestion. The reason, she hated to admit, had more to do with her and less to do with them.

"The thing is, I still have my freezing-up problem to contend with. If I don't return to the E.R., I'll never know for sure if I've conquered my fears." And it would be too easy after a year-and-a-half absence to stay away indefinitely.

"You don't think you'll have an opportunity to test yourself at the clinic?"

Aubrey recalled the day of her grandfather's first heart attack when she'd sat with her grandmother in the clinic. "I might."

"I hate to sound like a broken record, but become a medic with the Hotshots. I know the Sierra Nevada captain's been after you to do just that."

She rolled her eyes. "Your father would have a fit."

"What you do is none of his business."

"It's his business if I'm living on his ranch," she reiterated with a determined head shake. "I won't be the cause of more discord between the two of you."

They pulled into her grandmother's driveway, and Gage parked the truck near the front porch. There were more lights on in the house than Aubrey would have anticipated given the lateness of the hour, but she didn't pay much heed. Her mind was too preoccupied with Gage and their conversation.

He met her at the passenger door and enveloped her in a warm embrace. "Think about staying. That's all I ask."

Leaning down, he brushed her cheek with his. The slight

scratch of his five o'clock shadow reminded her of the many intimate pieces she'd felt that scratch during their recent lovemaking.

"We have a little time," he said. "You're not leaving for another two days." His voice was low and coaxing, the hand stroking her back soothing.

"Okay," she murmured.

"I'm serious, Aubrey. The situation's not perfect. But it's not permanent, either. Open yourself up to the possibilities before you say no. Surely there's a solution we can both agree on."

"I will think about it. I swear."

Like him, she wasn't ready to end their relationship. Truthfully, the only thing holding her back from accepting his proposition to move in with him was her reluctance to quit her job. That, more than the logistics of her staying, was what she needed to contemplate over the next two days.

"Will I see you tomorrow?" she asked.

"I'll call you sometime around lunch when I get a break."

At the front door, Gage drew her close. His tongue traced the outline of her lips before delving deep inside her mouth and sampling every corner. She stood on her toes, linked her arms around his neck and moaned with contentment. All these years, she still hadn't grown tired of his kisses.

Dim voices floated to her from inside the house. Her grandmother must have fallen asleep in front of the TV.

Gage gave her yet another lingering goodbye kiss. At the rate they were going, he'd never make it back in his truck.

All at once, the porch light came on and the front door opened. A tall, dark figure appeared behind the screen door.

"Aubrey? Is that you?"

She and Gage sprung apart. Momentarily disoriented, Aubrey didn't recognize the man at first. Then she did and her heart, already beating fast from kissing Gage, skipped erratically.

"Dad!"

"Don't act so shocked to see me."

"Well…I…" How could she not act shocked when he was the last person she'd expected to see tonight?

"Hello, Gage. Nice to see you again."

"Good evening, Dr. Stuart."

"How's your family?"

"Fine, thanks."

Neither man's demeanor held any discernable warmth, which did nothing to calm Aubrey's jangled nerves.

"What are you doing here, Dad?" Instantly self-conscious, she smoothed her hair. She vaguely pondered why she hadn't noticed her parents' Lexus and figured they must have parked it behind her SUV.

"Your mother and I came up to check on your grandmother."

"Oh. Okay."

He opened the screen door and gestured her and Gage inside. "And to drive with you back to Tucson."

Chapter Thirteen

"I've missed you."

Aubrey went through the front door and into her father's arms. "I've missed you, too."

Gage followed her inside, ignoring the laserlike glare searing into the back of his head.

Dr. Alexander Stuart hadn't exactly rejoiced when he learned about Aubrey's and Gage's elopement ten years ago. He'd wanted her to finish medical school before settling down. And while Gage never truly believed he'd intentionally sabotaged his and Aubrey's fledgling marriage—not consciously, anyway—he was relatively sure Dr. Stuart had breathed a very big sigh of relief when the divorce came through.

"Darling. You're back. Mother told us you went on a picnic. How nice." Carol May Stuart floated up from the couch with the grace and elegance of a swan taking flight.

Watching her, Gage found it hard to believe they shared the same humble beginnings. Not that he disliked his former mother-in-law. Far from it. While Carol May hadn't exactly welcomed him into the family fold, she hadn't opposed his and Aubrey's marriage, either.

"Hi, Mom." Aubrey met her mother in the center of the living room, and the two hugged fondly.

"Small-town living must suit you," Carol May gushed.

"You look wonderful. Doesn't she look wonderful, Alex?" Holding Aubrey's hand, she stepped back and beamed.

"She does indeed." Dr. Stuart's glance darted from Aubrey to Gage, and he shifted uncomfortably. Finding his ex-son-in-law on the front porch with his tongue halfway down his daughter's throat was probably just as awkward for him as it was for Gage.

Carol May tugged Aubrey toward the couch, where they both sat. "I can't believe how well Mother is doing." She cast a fond glance at Rose, who sat across from them in her favorite recliner.

"Aubrey's to be commended," Rose said. "She's a top-notch nurse."

Dr. Stuart moved to stand at the end of the couch beside Aubrey. A sentinel guarding the treasure, thought Gage. She'd told him her father hadn't wanted her to leave her job for six weeks and come to Blue Ridge. Was he afraid Gage might try and talk her into staying?

Well, hadn't he done exactly that? So, maybe Dr. Stuart did have a legit reason to worry.

"I can't take all the credit. Grandma is an easy patient."

"That's not what you told me last week," Rose complained with good-natured humor. "Or the week before."

Aubrey's posture relaxed for the first time since the porch light came on unexpectedly during her and Gage's kiss. "Well, there were days…"

"Gage, it's wonderful to see you again." Carol May aimed her radiant smile at him. "I hear you've become a wilderness firefighter."

"Yes, ma'am."

"He was promoted to crew leader today," Aubrey chimed in.

"Congratulations." Carol May appeared impressed.

Her husband less so. "That's a very dangerous occupation," Dr. Stuart said. "How does your mother feel about it?"

"She's pretty supportive, really." Gage studied the dynamics of the room and chose to stand by the side table near the entry, specifically because it put him opposite Dr. Stuart.

"And your father? Is he pretty supportive, too?"

"He's coming around." Gage would rip his fingernails out one by one with a pair of rusty pliers before discussing his family situation with Dr. Stuart.

"Hannah's attending Pineville College." Aubrey perched on the edge of her couch cushion. "She's taking over management of the ranch when she graduates."

Her efforts to diffuse the tension in the room were wasted. The invisible daggers shooting from one man to the other would fell anyone accidentally crossing the line of fire.

"Good for Hannah," Carol May said.

Small talk continued for the next twenty minutes, though Carol May, Aubrey and Rose dominated the conversation. When he wasn't being asked a question, Gage studied the Stuarts, Aubrey and her father in particular.

She loved him, that much was undeniable. And respected him. She also craved his approval, though if asked, she might deny it. But Gage knew Aubrey about as well as anyone did, and he'd witnessed her relationship with her father firsthand over the years. The once insecure little girl had grown into a woman who wanted to pick her own path, regardless of how her father felt or what, in his opinion, was best for her.

The trouble was, Dr. Stuart hadn't quite learned to let go.

Then again, Gage asked himself, was his relationship with his own father any different?

Not much.

When he and Aubrey eloped ten years ago, they should have stayed in Las Vegas and away from their dads. Maybe they'd still be married.

"Dolores Garcia announced she's retiring in two months," Dr. Stuart said abruptly.

"She is?" Aubrey swivelled on her cushion to stare up at her father with undisguised excitement.

"Really, Alex?" Carol May arched her delicately penciled eyebrows. "You didn't mention that on the ride up here."

"Who's Dolores Garcia?" Rose asked.

That's what Gage wanted to know, and why Aubrey seemed so fired up about her retirement.

"She's the nursing supervisor in the E.R." Dr. Stuart answered Rose, but it was Aubrey he looked at. "Been at Tucson General for twenty-something years."

"She's my boss," Aubrey clarified. She swung back around to face the room, though her attention was clearly elsewhere.

"I see." Gage's attention was also wandering, and he didn't like the direction it had taken.

"You need to put in your application right away." Dr. Stuart squeezed Aubrey's shoulder. "Your first day back at work. It's this Tuesday, right?"

Gage's head shot up. He waited for Aubrey to tell her father she was contemplating staying in Blue Ridge.

"Dad, I'm not qualified to be nursing supervisor. They won't give me the job."

She'd avoided the question, supporting Gage's bad feeling that more was happening than met the eye.

"No," Dr. Stuart concurred. "As head nurses, Clair Rittenbacher or Karen Karpinski will probably be recruited to replace her. But you *are* qualified for either of their positions," he added.

All at once the puzzle pieces clicked into place. Dr. Stuart hadn't made the trip to Blue Ridge solely to check on Rose. He had a second agenda, which was to facilitate Aubrey's return to her job so she could take that next important step up the career ladder.

Not altogether different from the night he'd shown up at the motor home, suggesting she return to school and switch her major to nursing, and he'd then provided her with the means to do it.

Gage's anger mounted. Aubrey talked by phone regularly with her family. Had Dr. Stuart noticed a recent change in his daughter's attitude? Or had he gotten wind from Carol May's conversations with Rose?

She fidgeted beneath Gage's scrutiny, unable or unwilling to offer a comment. And while it wasn't his place to speak for her, he was just mad enough at her father to overstep his boundaries.

"As it turns out," Gage said, "Aubrey might not be returning to Tucson. She's considering moving in with me."

"What!"

If Gage had been hoping to throw his former father-in-law for a loop, his plan was a rousing success.

"Is this true?" Dr. Stuart came around the corner of the couch to face Aubrey.

Seeking to restore the balance of power, Gage advanced several steps toward Aubrey.

"Why, that's wonderful," Rose exclaimed, the only person in the room besides Gage tickled at Aubrey's potential change of residence.

Aubrey certainly wasn't tickled. The frown she shot Gage shouted in no uncertain terms that she didn't appreciate his interference. Three seconds later he understood why.

"What the hell is wrong with you?" her father demanded.

"Dad—"

"You can't be seriously thinking of abandoning a promising career to live in this backwater town with him."

"Now, wait a minute, Alex." Carol May stiffened. "I was raised in this same backwater town."

"And fled the day you turned eighteen. Wisely, I might add." He ignored Rose's softly uttered protest.

Carol May didn't. "Was that necessary?"

"Whether I stay here or return to Tucson is my decision to make." Aubrey stood, her movements deliberate. "And I'll ask you to leave me to it."

Gage smiled. The Aubrey he'd known ten years ago didn't have the gumption to stand up to her father. Proud of her courage and maturity, he silently cheered her on.

Dr. Stuart, however, wasn't someone who relented easily and proceeded to make his case. "Head nurse would put you in a nice position for future promotions. Who knows when another opportunity like this one will come along?"

"You're right." Aubrey settled back on her heels. "Which is why I'll be returning to Tucson in two days. Not because it's what you want," she added, cutting off her father when he would have said more.

The smile on Gage's lips died. "What do you mean, returning to Tucson? Not thirty minutes ago you agreed to think seriously about staying in Blue Ridge."

"And I will." Conviction and determination were decidedly lacking in her voice.

Hope for a future with Aubrey seeped slowly out of Gage. He'd been a fool to believe he could counter Dr. Stuart's powers of persuasion. "It sounds to me like you've already decided."

She hesitated too long before answering. "Not…entirely."

Who was she kidding?

Who was *he* kidding? Aubrey might have toyed with the idea of moving in with him, but she was never serious about it. Not like him.

"I'm glad to see you're being sensible." Dr. Stuart visibly relaxed.

And why not? He'd won. Again.

Yet it was Aubrey and not her father Gage directed his anger at. She'd strung him along these past weeks, and, like an eager-to-please puppy, he'd obliged her. Fresh resentment mingled with a decade-old sense of betrayal.

"Have you ever seen a commitment through to the end?" he bit out. "Just once?"

She drew herself up in mild shock. "Excuse me?"

"You quit school when you were a freshman because you couldn't cope with the pressure and came running here. We get married and after six short weeks, you hightailed it back home the second Daddy came around and crooked his little finger."

"That's not true." Fists planted firmly on her hips, she stared at him with incredulity.

"How else would you describe it?"

"We were miserable."

"We were newlyweds. Adjusting to the change. And we weren't miserable every second." He could tell from the slight widening of her eyes she'd caught his meaning. "Then, two months ago, we have what amounts to the same scenario. Only instead of college, it's your job you can't handle. So, just like before, you leave Tucson and head here. Surprise, surprise, Daddy shows up, and he convinces you it's in your best interest to go back with him. Tell me I'm wrong."

"Can't handle your job? What's he talking about, Aubrey?" Carol May demanded. Clearly she hadn't been included in the loop regarding Aubrey's career crisis.

"My grandmother needed me," Aubrey said, addressing Gage, not her mother.

"Your grandmother needed a nurse. Not necessarily you." Somewhere in the back of his mind Gage realized he should shut up, but once started, he couldn't—or wouldn't—stop. His pain ran too deep, he hurt too much. "Face it, Aubrey, you grabbed the first available excuse to bail on another commitment. Just like you're doing tonight."

"You're…wrong."

"Is having a relationship with me really that scary?"

"Of course not."

"Why don't I believe you?"

She pushed an unruly lock of hair back from her face with unnecessary impatience. "You know how important my career is to me and how few job options there are for nurses in Blue Ridge."

"You couldn't wait eighteen months? I said I'd move to Tucson when Hannah graduated."

"The emergency department at Tucson General isn't all that big," Dr. Stuart interjected. "There may not be another head nurse position open for years. If you care about her, you won't hold her back."

"He's pressuring you into leaving, Aubrey," Gage said. "Can't you see it?"

"He's not the only one," she snapped. "*You're* pressuring me into staying."

"Like I pressured you into marriage? Like your father pressured you to go back to school and is doing essentially the same thing now with your job? Can't you ever make up your own mind about anything?"

"I…" Her face crumbled, proof his accusations stung.

Gage sighed. He'd made his point, but the victory was hollow. "All I asked you for was two days. Two days to consider the possibilities. You didn't last an hour."

Carol May rose from the couch. "Why don't we retire to the kitchen and give Aubrey and Gage some privacy." Over her shoulder she said, "Alex?"

He didn't budge.

"Don't bother." Gage whirled around and headed for the front door. Privacy wasn't going to help resolve the problems between him and Aubrey. At this point, nothing would.

She followed him to the door. "Gage. Wait…"

He stopped and stared down at her. "Give me one reason to."

She was so pretty. And vulnerable. He could see she hated the fact they were arguing, and it tore him up inside. Yet as mad as he was, if she gave even the tiniest indication she'd stay, he'd sweep her in his arms, kiss her soundly and forget their fight ever happened.

She wasn't about to do any such thing. He could see that, too.

"You're being stubborn." She sniffed, blinked back tears.

"Yeah, I am. You know why? Because I want all of you. Not just the part your dad isn't controlling."

"What about your dad? He controls you."

"He sure as hell tries to. But the difference between you and me is I recognize it, admit it, and am doing my dead level best to fight it." He pushed open the screen door and hit the porch.

"My dad is right about some things," she called after him.

Gage stopped at the bottom step but didn't turn around.

"Becoming a nurse was a good career choice me," she said to his back. "And we weren't ready for marriage."

He rubbed his neck, which was stiff and sore. "Doesn't appear like we're any more ready now."

She opened the screen door and stepped out onto the porch. "I'm sorry."

Before he could respond, his radio went off. He listened to the dispatch, then reached for his cell phone.

"Gage?"

"I have to go," he said and jogged to his truck.

For the first time since running into Aubrey two months ago at the convenience store in Pineville, he was glad to be called to a fire.

On impulse, Aubrey pulled the twin bed she'd been sleeping in the past two months away from the wall. With one hand on the windowsill, she bent and peered into the narrow space she'd created between the wall and the wooden headboard. What she saw brought a smile to her lips and bittersweet sadness to her heart.

There, lined up in a not quite straight row, were fourteen *X*s carved into the back of the headboard. One for each summer she and Annie had stayed with their grandparents. It had been a tradition for the girls to carve a new *X* on the matching twin headboards their last day there before starting the drive home.

Since the marks weren't rubbed out or painted over, Grandma Rose must not have found them. That, or she treasured them with the same sentimentality as Aubrey.

She was tempted to carve another *X*, one for this summer, then chided herself for her silliness. She wasn't a kid anymore. And Annie wasn't with her to make a game of the ritual.

Besides, marking the headboard would be admitting she was really and truly leaving Blue Ridge…and Gage.

Aubrey and her parents were scheduled to depart in less than an hour, and she still wasn't fully convinced she was doing the right thing.

Everyone she ran into yesterday asked her why she was leaving and wished her good luck in a singsong voice suggesting she'd need it where she was going.

Did they know something she didn't?

"Aubrey?" Grandma Rose tapped lightly on the door.

"Yeah. Just a minute." Aubrey climbed awkwardly to her feet. Butting her legs against the footboard, she pushed the small bed back into place and winced guiltily at the loud scraping noise. "Hey," she said, flinging the door open. "What's up?"

"Everything all right?" Grandma Rose studied Aubrey's face.

"Fine."

"You look flushed."

"Oh." Aubrey dismissed her grandmother with what she hoped passed for a nonchalant laugh and gestured her into the bedroom. "I was crawling around behind the bed looking for any forgotten items."

And she'd found some. Fourteen *X*s.

"Is this a bad time?" Grandma Rose asked.

"No, not at all." Aubrey smiled. She'd been smiling a lot the last day or so, and it had yet to feel natural.

Grandma Rose perched on the edge of the bed. "I have something for you."

"What's that?" Aubrey sat down beside her.

Souvenirs were another farewell tradition. Grandma Rose would present Aubrey and her sister with a token gift their last morning in Blue Ridge. It was never much. Just a little memento to remind them of the summer.

"Here." Grandma Rose reached into the pocket of her floral smock and withdrew a small object. "I've been waiting for the right moment to give this to you."

The gift was hardly token and not what Aubrey expected. Her grandmother placed it in her hands, prompting a protest.

"I can't accept this."

"Why not?"

"It's too special." Emotion caused her throat to close.

Housed inside the antique sterling-silver frame was a black-and-white photograph of Grandma Rose and Grandpa Glen taken more than fifty years earlier on their honeymoon in San Francisco. Arms linked and dressed smartly in the fashion of the day, they stood on a grassy knoll. Behind them, stretching endlessly, was a magnificent view of Golden Gate Bridge. And yet, they had eyes only for each other.

The photograph had occupied a corner of her Grandma Rose's dresser since shortly after it was taken, and Aubrey knew her grandmother cherished the keepsake.

"Which is why I want you to have it," Grandma Rose insisted. "I'm getting older and there's too much stuff in this house for me to take care of. With my bum hip, I need to lighten my housework."

Aubrey couldn't imagine how much extra housework one little framed photograph could cause. She mentally placed her and Gage in the picture, calculating how old they would be if their marriage had lasted fifty years. But then, they didn't have a photograph from their honeymoon, mostly because they'd never gone on one. Not a real honeymoon, leastwise. Unless an overnight stay in a cheap Las Vegas hotel counted.

It seemed to Aubrey that the cosmos was forever conspiring against them. Each time they came close to making a life together, something intervened.

Something? Or *someone?*

"Grandma," she said, "do you think I let Dad control me?"

"Well…" Her grandmother pursed her lips thoughtfully. "I'm not sure I'd put it that way."

Half annoyed and half intrigued, Aubrey asked, "What way would you put it?"

"You're very bright and talented. Always have been. People like you are expected to do well. Be incredibly successful. Problem is, parents of bright and talented children can do them a disservice. They see the potential, are proud of it and push their offspring too hard."

"Like Dad?"

"He can be a force to be reckoned with when he wants to."

"Which is most of the time." Aubrey thought back on her relationship with her father, attempting to look at it from a different angle. "You think I'm afraid of failing?"

"And of letting your father down."

"Sounds like classic first-born syndrome to me."

"It does."

Aubrey had intended to be funny but her grandmother obviously took her seriously, which sobered Aubrey.

"Oh, I'm not saying you haven't ever rebelled," Grandma Rose continued. "You did that just recently by coming here when he wanted to hire someone."

"But I haven't exactly cut the apron strings, either," Aubrey said glumly.

She traced a finger back and forth across the photograph of her grandparents, thinking more of her love for Gage than her somewhat dysfunctional relationship with her father.

The pink-and-turquoise Barbie phone on the small desk started ringing. Grandma Rose creaked to a standing position and went to answer it. When Aubrey first arrived two months ago, she'd been surprised and amused that the once adored possession still functioned.

"Hello. Oh, hi, Eleanor." Grandma Rose nodded at Aubrey. "She's still here. Do you want to talk to—" Deep creases formed in her grandmother's brow. "What's that?"

Several seconds passed during which her grandmother's concern visibly increased. Aubrey set the photograph on the nightstand and went to stand near her.

"Thank you for calling, Eleanor. I appreciate it." Grandma Rose hung up the phone and turned to Aubrey. "The fire changed direction during the night. It's fifteen miles east of Blue Ridge and heading this way."

"What!" Aubrey struggled to digest the unexpected news. "It was thirty miles away and headed in the opposite direction when we went to bed last night."

"Apparently the wind changed course around midnight."

"Oh, my God."

Shock set in as Aubrey realized the seriousness of the situation. She ran to the window behind her bed and pushed aside the curtain. Smoke filled the distant sky, hanging low over the hilltops and shining an eerie incandescent silver in the early morning light. Fear seizing her, she stumbled away from the bed.

"I have to go tell Mom and Dad. No way are we leaving now. Did Eleanor recommend you evacuate?"

"Not yet. She said she'd keep everyone advised of the fire's status."

"Still, I think we should prepare for the possibility. Fifteen miles isn't that far."

How was Gage doing, she wondered, and what was he feeling having to fight a fire so close to his hometown? Something her grandmother said about the direction of the fire suddenly penetrated her brain and triggered a rush of alarm.

"The Raintree ranch is east of Blue Ridge. At the rate the fire's traveling, it could reach there in a matter of hours!"

"Dear heaven."

"I think I'll call Susan. Ask if she needs any help."

Before Aubrey could pick up the phone, it rang again. Grandma Rose answered it.

"Hello. Yes, just a moment." She passed the phone to Aubrey, her eyes solemn. "It's someone named Larry Newcombe. Says he's a commander with the wilderness firefighters."

A dozen questions raced through Aubrey's mind in the three seconds it took her to place the phone to her ear, most of them centering on Gage and whether or not he was safe and unharmed.

"This is Aubrey Stuart," she said in a tight voice.

Commander Newcombe didn't waste time with a greeting. "I hope you don't mind me contacting you at home, Ms.

Stuart. We were in contact with the local authorities and they gave us your name and number." He cleared his throat. "We need your help."

"My help? How?"

"We're short medics and injuries have been heavier than usual. The BLM and Forest Service are flying some more in, but they won't arrive until this afternoon."

"I see."

"Is there any chance you can come?"

Weeks of resistance to the idea of volunteering with the Hotshots vanished in a flash. "Of course, I'll be there as quickly as I can."

"Thank you, ma'am. We sure appreciate it."

She gave the commander her cell phone number, then opened the desk drawer and removed a pad of paper and pen. "I'll need directions."

"Fire camp is on Verde Road, about four miles south of where it junctions with the highway. Look for the markers. Once you arrive in camp, we'll transport you to the front line."

Front line? The term sounded scarily like warfare to Aubrey. "How close will I be to the fire?"

"A mile or two."

Aubrey swallowed.

"I take it you've been recruited," Grandma Rose said when Aubrey disconnected with the commander.

"Appears so." Folding the paper with the directions and stuffing it in her pocket, Aubrey filled her grandmother in on the details as best she knew them.

"How long will you be away?"

"I don't know." Aubrey shrugged. "As long as they need me, I suppose."

"You be careful."

"You, too. And call Susan for me if you don't mind." Together they left the bedroom and went in search of her parents. "The folks will evacuate you if it comes to that. And speaking of the folks…"

Aubrey sighed. She didn't figure her parents would be happy with the news or the least bit understanding. Her father especially.

To her utter and complete astonishment, she was wrong.

"Naturally, you must go," her mother said when Aubrey finished explaining to her parents about Commander Newcombe's phone call. "I'll contact the hospital for you, explain your delay."

Aubrey's mother been doing laundry most of the morning, catching it up for Grandma Rose before they left. Clean clothing and linens were folded and stacked in neat piles on the kitchen table, filling every available space.

"Thanks, Mom." Aubrey gathered her purse and a few personal necessities she thought she might need. Spying the clean laundry, she decided a change of clothing was in order. And sturdier shoes. Turning in a half circle, she made a beeline back to her bedroom, where she'd left her packed suitcases.

A few minutes later, her father met her on the porch and walked her to her SUV. "You say the Hotshots are understaffed?"

"That's what I'm told." Aubrey opened the driver's side door and tossed her tote bag onto the passenger seat.

Admittedly, she'd been a little cool to her father since the other night, though she couldn't blame him entirely for what had happened. He might have been the catalyst for her and Gage's argument but not the cause of it, in spite of what Gage claimed.

She had only herself to blame for that fiasco.

"Wait a minute, Aubrey," he said when she would have escaped into the SUV.

Expecting a lecture, she cut him short. Her father was *not* going to talk her out of helping the Hotshots. "Dad, I need to leave. Now." In the short time it had taken her to get ready to leave, the columns of smoke had doubled in size.

"Do you…" Her father hesitated, something he rarely did. "Do you think the Hotshots could use a doctor, as well as a nurse?"

"What?" She was tempted to glance at the sky and see if it had fallen. Surely she'd heard wrong.

"If they're short of medical help, they could probably—"

"Are you serious?"

"Well…yes. I've already spoken to your mother. She'll drive your grandmother to a motel in Pineville if the authorities recommend evacuating Blue Ridge."

Stupefied, Aubrey stared. Her father, the great Alexander Stuart, heart surgeon *extraordinaire,* had just offered to help treat firefighters under conditions that were bound to be harsh and with equipment that, compared to the ultramodern operating room he was accustomed to, could only be called primitive.

"Wow." She blinked and when he didn't disappear, she smiled.

"Is that a yes?"

"An unequivocal yes!" Leaping into his arms, she hugged him fiercely. "Thank you, Daddy." Abruptly, she pushed away from him and frowned. "Do you still remember basic triage?"

"Get in the car," he said gruffly, giving her a playful shove. "And quit picking on your old man." He went around to the passenger door. "I'll have you know I could outsuture you with one hand tied behind my back."

"Just checking." Laughing, she started the engine and passed him the paper with the scribbled directions. "Here. You be navigator."

Their camaraderie lasted for several miles. Aubrey had never worked with her father before and discovered she eagerly anticipated the opportunity. Or was it practicing emergency nursing again after a too-long absence that had her blood pumping and her nerves tingling? Except for when she and Gage were making love, she hadn't felt this alive, this excited, since leaving Tucson. In hindsight, she'd been wrong not to accept Captain Greenough's invitation and become a volunteer medic when he first asked her.

Could this be the happy medium she and Gage were searching for the other night?

The question and its possibly significant answer were instantly forgotten as Aubrey and her father rounded a bend and reached a large clearing.

The entire mountainside glowed a fiery orange. Smoke rose from the tops of the flames in giant, fluffy white columns that seemed to tower as high as the clouds themselves. In the wake of the flames lay acres upon acres of scorched landscape.

Aubrey hit the brakes and parked the SUV. For several moments, she and her father stared in stunned silence.

"Good Lord," she said, her voice scratchy from having been temporarily silent.

Her father grunted and cleared his throat. "If there really is a hell on Earth, I do believe we're looking at it."

His sentiment matched her feelings exactly. She pressed the accelerator and resumed driving, thinking not of herself and her father, but of the perils Gage and all the Hotshots faced while fighting this unholy monster.

Chapter Fourteen

"Ready?"

"Almost." In response to her father's cue, Aubrey lowered herself to the ground in front of the injured firefighter.

The man, a burly ten-year veteran who looked strong enough to bench-press a tree trunk, lay in one of two cots set up in the medical tent. He'd been brought in about an hour earlier with a dislocated pinky. The affected finger stuck out from his hand at a ninety-degree angle and probably hurt like the dickens—or had hurt until the Novocain her father administered took effect a few minutes ago.

"You hanging in there?" Aubrey asked. Draping an arm over the upper half of his body, she leaned close.

"I think so." The man grinned and the dirt caking his face cracked in several places. "Could be worse. You're a lot prettier than the last medic who patched me up."

He smelled of smoke and sweat, though it was hardly noticeable over the acrid odor of burning wilderness. The smoke was inescapable, even at a distance of two miles from the fire. It permeated the air, causing Aubrey's eyes to sting and her lungs to burn.

Blinking back tears, she unbuttoned the man's yellow fire-retardant shirt in order to ease his breathing. Earlier she'd removed his hard hat, setting it on the ground next to his equipment pack.

"Should I bite down on a stick or something?" the man asked.

Aubrey returned his grin. "Only if you want to."

"You think I'm kidding, don't you?" His laugh deteriorated into a hacking cough.

Since their arrival sometime around nine, she and her father had worked nonstop. When Aubrey last checked her watch, it was almost four. Lunch, consisting of a protein drink, was gulped down between two bee-sting victims and a severe case of friction blisters.

Some of the firefighters, like the one suffering dehydration, had received rudimentary first aid from a medic on the line before being transported to their medical tent, a short fifteen-minute drive from the blaze. The more seriously afflicted firefighters, and Aubrey understood from snatches of various conversations she overheard there'd been a few, were flown directly to the hospital in Pineville or, if need be, as far as Phoenix.

The noise was relentless. People shouting, trucks roaring, the wind whistling and aircraft buzzing.

She'd witnessed the helicopters, zipping back and forth like giant insects, pouring water on the fire, airlifting firefighters to and from the fire, and transporting cargo. Planes—tankers she'd been told—also flew overhead, dropping brightly colored fire retardant from compartments in their bellies and missing the helicopters by mere inches.

The fire had started three days ago, the result of a lightning strike. While it had claimed nearly a thousand acres of land, lives and property were thus far spared. Talk among the firefighters was that could change—and possibly soon would—if the Smokejumpers, Hotshots, Helitack and Engine crews weren't able to stop the blaze from heading into Blue Ridge. The Hotshots and other ground crews were on a race against the clock, attempting to cut a line around the perimeter of the fire that, God willing, would hold and save the town.

Wind, the same one that had caused the fire to change

course during the night, presented the greatest danger. It had picked up speed, with gusts reaching forty-five miles per hour. Sparks and flying debris were starting new fires so fast, the firefighters weren't able keep pace. Aubrey didn't understand all the terms and jargon being bantered about, but she picked up enough to ascertain the people in charge were worried.

That worry was contagious.

Every second Aubrey's mind wasn't focused on a patient, she was thinking of Gage and praying for his well-being. She would have liked to check in with her mother, but her cell phone didn't work, not that she'd found a spare second to place a call.

Her father rose to a half-standing position, braced their patient's hand in his lap and, using his weight, popped the pinky back into its socket.

"Is it over?" The man looked questioningly at Aubrey, who'd positioned herself to block his view of the procedure. Sweat beaded his upper lip, more likely the result of nervousness than pain.

"Not quite." She patted his shoulder and stood. "But the hard part's over. You just take it easy while I get you some ibuprofen."

No sooner did she turn than the wind blew so hard, the nylon tent rattled and shook, the entry flaps snapping like flags mounted to a parade vehicle. The gust didn't let up and continued to pummel the tent with blasts of hot, stale air.

Icy chills danced up Aubrey's spine. An overwhelming sense of dread accompanied the chill, and Aubrey shivered.

Gage!

She couldn't explain how she knew, but something was wrong. Terribly, frighteningly, wrong. Her feet cemented to the ground, she went from shivering to shaking. The background noise grew in volume, becoming unbearable. She covered her ears, remembering the night her Uncle Jesse and Aunt Maureen were brought into the E.R.

"Aubrey, sweetheart. Are you okay?" Her father came up behind her.

"Dad…" She let him hold her, but it didn't quell her shaking.

"Hey," the injured man called from the cot. "What's going on?"

At that moment, the tent flaps were shoved aside and a grim-faced firefighter entered. "Wanted to give you folks a heads-up. We just received an alert from command post. There's a dry cold front moving in. Could mean trouble of the big variety. Prepare for incoming, just in case." As quickly as he arrived, he left.

"Incoming?" Aubrey asked. "Like in injuries and casualties?"

"Yeah," her father answered, as serious as the firefighter had been. "We'd better hop to it."

Aubrey's last thoughts before sprinting into action were of Gage and how she wished their last words hadn't been angry ones.

"THIS ISN'T THE PLACE I would've picked to make a stand." Gage straightened, ignored the arrows of pain shooting up both sides of his back, and stabbed the axe end of his Pulaski into the ground.

"Yeah, well, sometimes we don't get to pick." Marty re-attached his radio to the front of his jacket. "The fire does it for us."

The Hotshots had been hard at it, cutting a fire line since sunup. On the hill opposite them, across a narrow ravine, flames devoured everything in their path, impervious to the war being waged against them. Starved for water after a dry summer, the brittle vegetation supplied the perfect fuel.

Low-flying tankers dropped retardant, covering the un-touched landscape with a blanket of red chemical powder. While bulldozers toppled trees and brush, lumberjacks wielded chainsaws, providing a solid second line of defense. Ground crews, Gage's among them, provided the first—a backfire they'd set hours earlier in the hopes of halting the fire by forcing a convection column.

If their cumulative efforts failed, the results could prove to be the most disastrous wild land fire in the state's history.

Command post had just called, warning them of the approaching cold front and accompanying high winds. Of all the news they could have received, it was without a doubt the worst. Gage's bones, already weary well past the point of exhaustion, tingled with a sense of foreboding.

For ten straight hours, he and his crew had been pounding the ground, with only periodic ten-minute breaks—and that was just today. Yesterday, they were at it for fourteen straight hours. The day before was a blur, beginning around 11:00 p.m. when he left Aubrey standing on the porch of her grandmother's house and ending some twenty-four hours later when he and his crew lay down to sleep in the dirt of the fire line they'd just dug.

Six hours later, they were up and at it again, cutting trees, scraping earth and burning safety zones. Somewhere or other, there'd been a second short snooze, Gage couldn't remember when.

The fire had started out small. Didn't they all? And until this morning they'd foolishly believed it would be quickly contained.

They were wrong.

By midmorning, what had been a gentle breeze progressed into a strong wind. That was when all hell started to break loose. The cold front, however, would make the wind look like a sneeze in comparison.

The firefighters, over a hundred in all counting three Hotshots squads, Smokejumpers, one Navajo crew and one inmate crew, had been ordered to take a stand. A different location, one less susceptible, would have been preferred. Time and the weather denied them the luxury of choosing.

They either stopped the fire at this steep, rocky slope or the flames would roar right over them, pushed by the relentless wind. The first privately owned land the fire would reach belonged to Gage's family. The town of Blue Ridge lay eight miles beyond that.

He hoped to hell his father and Hannah had moved the herds to the west pasture. The cows would move themselves when confronted with a fire and likely scatter. They could get stuck in a gully or run into a fence. Either situation spelled the end to both their lives and the Raintree finances.

Had Aubrey left for Tucson yet? Gage wondered. Was it even today she was supposed to leave? He'd lost track of the date, measuring the passage of time by the Hotshots' progress, not hours or minutes.

God, he was tired

"Call the crew together." Marty's order shattered Gage's momentary lapse of concentration.

The Blue Ridge Hotshots took a short reprieve from their labors to discuss strategy and determine the fastest escape route to their safety zone. Should there be a blowup, a very real possibility with the wind acting like the inside of a blender on high speed, Gage wanted every one of them to make it out in one piece.

Their weariness forgotten, the crew returned to work with renewed gusto. Arms resembling the pistons of a finely tuned machine, axes, shovels, and Pulaskis hit the ground in rapid fire succession. Foot by foot, they cut a line, trying their damnedest to reach the Navajo crew on the lower end of the slope and close the gap before the fire crossed the ravine.

Sweat dripped from every pore, soaking their grime-encrusted clothing. What were, in reality, forty-pound equipment packs felt as if they weighed a hundred and forty. Smoke, thick and foul, breeched their protective equipment, seeping into their lungs. Breathing became sheer agony.

Still, the Hotshots kept digging. Nothing would stop them, not when the enemy continued to advance.

So much was at risk—so much depended on them—and the Hotshots took the responsibility personally. Gage more than the others. This wasn't just any town, any people. Blue Ridge was his home, the lives in jeopardy those of his friends and family.

All at once, the Navajo crew members were practically beside them. Positioned at the end of the Blue Ridge line, Gage signaled with a raised hand. The Navajo crew member nearest to him pointed. Gage looked up, and his superheated blood instantly froze.

The fire had vaulted across the narrow ravine, propelled by the strong, oxygen-rich wind. Before his eyes, the fire caught and grew to an amazing size. Like a giant emerging from the entrance to hell, it funneled up the hill toward them. In its wake lay a wide path of burning trees and brush.

Gage hollered a warning to his crew, who simultaneously raised their heads. Until that moment, they'd had their noses to the grindstone, focused exclusively on digging the line. Several of the men shielded their faces with their forearms and stepped back. One crossed himself.

Suddenly, the fire exploded into a tower of flames a hundred feet tall. Bits of fiery debris rained down, igniting small fires every place they landed. If the Hotshots didn't get the hell out of there, they'd be dead.

"Run!" Gage shouted. He didn't have to give the order twice.

Breaking formation, his crew dropped their tools and scrambled up the slope toward the safety zone on top. The Navajo crew had the same idea and were one step ahead of the Blue Ridge Hotshots.

Gage knew he should follow. There was nothing in his training or his past experiences that didn't scream at him to run for his life. But ten feet of ground remained open. It could be insignificant—it could also be the gate through which the fire passed.

Remote as that possibility was, he couldn't take the chance.

His Pulaski slammed into the ground again and again until his chest ached and his arms trembled. He didn't realize for some seconds he had company. Marty worked beside him.

"You're an idiot," Gage screamed at him.

"Takes one to know one."

Another minute flew by. They closed the gap to five feet. Two. Then it happened. An invisible wave of heat blasted them, throwing them backward. Gage glanced up and stared into a mammoth wall of fire—what some called the mouth of the dragon.

"Shit!"

His knees buckled, his insides clenched. He wasn't ashamed to admit he'd been scared plenty during his career as a firefighter. All those times rolled into one didn't match the terror gripping him now.

Twisting sideways, he shoved Marty. Hard. "Move!"

They sprinted up the slope, the fire chasing them. Flames blistered their backsides, licked their clothing. Whether they dropped their equipment packs or the fire burned through the straps, Gage wasn't sure. The lack of extra weight proved a blessing.

"Go, go, go!"

Fingers clawing at any available handhold, feet grappling for traction, they half ran, half crawled. And still, the fire kept coming. Fast. So fast. Through watery eyes, Gage saw the top of the slope where his crew waited. He and Marty were almost there. Incredibly, they'd gained a few yards on the fire.

Then, without warning, the earth beneath them collapsed. Marty stumbled and bowled into Gage, knocking his legs out from under him. Gage pitched forward and landed on his face. He began to slide. Whatever air his lungs held whooshed out. Dirt filled his mouth. His vision blurred. Dimmed. Pain seized his limbs, immobilizing them.

He lay there, unable to do more than breathe the dragon's poisonous fumes, absorb its searing heat.

Aubrey's face appeared before him, first in a younger incarnation, then as she looked today.

Gage grunted. He wasn't ready to die, not by a long shot. But unlike the movies, the revelation didn't miraculously empower him with the strength to rise and stagger that last little bit to safety.

It did, however, fill him with the determination to hang on, something someone was yelling at him to do if his cotton-plugged ears were hearing right.

Yeah, hang on. If only to see Aubrey again and apologize for their stupid fight. Afterward, he'd drop to his knees and tell her he loved her. Tell her he didn't give a rat's ass about her father or his father or his job or anything else getting between them and a lifetime of happiness together. He'd move with her to Tucson. Hell, he'd move with her to the dark side of the moon if that's where she wanted to live.

For twenty-four years, since the day he met her in Sunday school, she'd been the only one for him. The love of his life. A ten-year separation hadn't lessened his feelings for her. Nothing would. Certainly not this fire.

A hand clamped around his right wrist and pulled. Another hand grabbed his left wrist. Still another hand grabbed him by his shirt collar. Gage was dragged over dirt and rocks and small sticks poking up from the ground. He thought his stomach and the side of his face might be permanently scraped off, though he didn't complain. Had he been able to speak, he would have thanked his buddies for coming to his rescue.

God willing, they had Marty, too. He figured they did. Any firefighter worth their salt would cut off their arm before leaving one of their crew behind.

Gage tried to move but someone placed a restraining hand on him.

"Christ, Raintree. You and Paxton scared the crap out of us."

The voice belonged to Freddy Gomez, a rookie Gage thought showed real promise. If the kid returned next summer after surviving this fire, they'd know for sure he was crazy like the rest of them.

"Get 'em some water," someone hollered.

In the next instant, a canteen was placed to Gage's mouth. He tried to drink. Most of the water spilled down his chin and neck and into his shirt, which, considering how hot he was, didn't feel half bad. Hands fumbled with the buttons of his shirt and breathing became a little easier. Fingers pushed a tablet into his mouth and the taste of salt exploded on his tongue. His headgear was removed, and a cold pack was placed on his forehead. Gage wanted to whimper with gratitude.

"Let's go."

Go where? Gage vaguely wondered. Thinking coherently had become a real nuisance, so he stop trying.

There was a rush of movement and he was suddenly suspended in midair. For an instant he panicked until he realized his men were carrying him. He tried to open his eyes but they were sealed shut. Swollen, he hoped, not burned. Had he lost his goggles? He couldn't recall. His ears appeared to function well enough, though what was being said sounded garbled.

"Radio in for a helicopter."

"Screw the copter. Not enough time. There's an engine on top. Let's load 'em in that. Road 128 is clear."

"Where's the closest medic station?"

"I'll find out."

Gage relaxed. Marty was alive, too, or the guys wouldn't be in such a rush to transport the two of them to help.

His peace of mind didn't last. Constant jostling took a toll on him in the form of nausea and a throbbing headache. He fought the urge to vomit by biting down on the insides of his cheeks. When he felt himself being loaded into the back of the engine, the nausea eased but not the dizziness. The engine roared to life and in the next minute, he was riding the world's fastest merry-go-round with no pole on which to cling.

Someone laid a damp cloth over his face to block the sun. Gage sighed and let go, drifting into a state halfway between consciousness and unconsciousness. His last lucid thought was of the line they'd dug and whether or not it would hold.

Chapter Fifteen

Onlookers stared as the bright yellow Forest Service engine barreled down the gravel road, kicking up a miniwhirlwind of dust and pebbles. Aubrey clamped her teeth together and grimaced when the driver took the last curve at a speed far exceeding what any sane person would deem safe.

"Here they come," her father said. Picking up one of the lightweight stretchers, he began walking.

Aubrey grabbed the second stretcher and hurried after him. They knew only that two injured firefighters were being brought in, victims of a blowup.

Injured, she reminded herself. *Not dead. Not yet.*

And not if she could help it.

Keep it together, Aubrey. Don't freeze.

Since receiving the radio alert advising them of the injured firefighters, she'd been battling anxiety, acutely aware of her father's presence. Embarrassment at freezing up was a minor concern. Failing a patient was an altogether different matter.

She was an E.R. nurse, good at what she did. Better than good. At least that much was true until the night her Uncle Jesse and Aunt Maureen died. The past two months had been a cakewalk for Aubrey. Working in the clinic, helping at the community center, hadn't exactly put her competency in a crisis to the test.

Not like today.

Her nerves stretched tighter with each step she took as visions of charred flesh filled her mind. She willed the grisly images away.

Should the firefighters be suffering from third degree burns, they'd need every ounce of her skill. This was not the time to fall to pieces.

You can do it, Aubrey.

Amid a cacophony of grinding gears and squealing brakes, the engine skidded to a stop beside two other vehicles. Men piled out from inside the cab, scrambled down from on top and leapt off from the sides where they'd been hanging.

"Medic!" one of them shouted.

Aubrey and her father broke into awkward trots, hampered by the portable stretchers.

Two men remained on top while the rest gathered at the back of the engine. They were sweaty and filthy, barely discernable as human. One of the guys on the ground turned sideways, then another.

Aubrey's steps faltered. So did her heart.

"You all right?" Her father spared her a quick glance over his shoulder.

"Fine."

But she wasn't fine. She recognized the name printed on the men's helmets. Her eyes went straight to their face. She recognized them, too. In the three weeks she and Gage dated, she'd met most of the Blue Ridge Hotshots.

More familiar faces appeared as equipment and protective clothing were discarded.

Where was Gage?

Trotting faster, Aubrey scanned the group, her concern escalating to fear as she studied and dismissed each firefighter in turn.

No Gage.

Where the hell was he?

Don't jump to conclusions, she cautioned herself and promptly refused to heed her own advice.

Her father reached the engine ahead of her. A firefighter offered to take the stretcher from her and she let him, reminding herself that the injured men would have been flown to the nearest hospital if their condition was critical.

Relax. Keep moving.

Why wasn't Gage with his crew?

The firefighters crowded in around Aubrey and her father. Voices merged, and she had trouble deciphering them. An icy sensation formed in her middle and radiated outward, pooling in her fingers and toes. Her movements slowed, became sluggish, hampered by her lead-weighted limbs.

It was the night her Uncle Jesse and Aunt Maureen died all over again.

Not now. Please!

"Give us some room," her father shouted.

He was instantly obeyed, and a hole opened. Four firefighters stood ready with the stretchers.

"Stand by." Her father climbed on the back of the engine and motioned with his hand. "Lower them down."

Aubrey held her breath and stared as the first casualty was gingerly placed on a waiting stretcher and strapped in.

Marty! She recognized him immediately. And he was all right! Talking, in fact.

Fists balled at her sides and feet rooted to the ground, she watched them load the second man onto the remaining stretcher. A cloth covered his face, preventing her from identifying him. Her father hopped off the engine and bent over the man, removing the cloth.

The entire right side of his face was scraped and bleeding. So were his hands, she noticed. Sweat had matted his hair to his head, and his eyes were swollen shut. Beneath numerous layers of dirt, his exposed skin shone bright red.

He didn't move, not even when one of the firefighters accidentally bumped the stretcher. Not even when her father spoke into his ear.

Aubrey, however, did move. Like lightning.

"Let me through!"

Plowing into the small crowd, she pushed and shoved her way to his side.

"Is he alive?"

Dear Lord, she never dreamed there'd be a day when she'd have to ask that question about Gage.

"Yeah, he's alive," a young man Aubrey thought was called Freddy answered. He carried the front end of Gage's stretcher. "Just got the shit banged out of him. Marty, too."

She could see that for herself.

Picking up one of Gage's battered hands, she clasped it in hers. His flesh was warm. Gloriously, wonderfully warm.

Then again, maybe too warm. He must be burning up inside.

Her father offered a more detailed medical assessment than Freddy's as they walked the stretchers toward the tent. Aubrey let her gaze wander over Gage, mentally concurring.

"What happened?"

She suppressed a shudder as the tale of the unexpected blowup was recounted along with Gage and Marty's valiant efforts to close the line. They were damn lucky to get out of there, damn lucky to have a crew willing to risk their lives to rescue them.

"Put them on the cots," her father ordered once they entered the tent. "And easy does it. Aubrey, I'll get the IVs started. You prep the patients."

Hydrating Gage and Marty and lowering their body temperatures were the number-one priorities. Lacking a pole, Aubrey's father handed the IV bags to the two closest firefighters, one being Freddy.

"Keep these well above their heads at all times."

Using a pair of scissors, Aubrey cut off Marty's shirt and then Gage's, leaving them both bare to the waist.

Given the events immediately preceding the blowup, they were probably suffering from smoke inhalation and heat exhaustion. Possibly heatstroke. Their exact prognosis wouldn't be fully determined until she and her father had finished conducting thorough examinations.

Marty was awake and alert, correctly answering the questions put to him. She wished Gage would rouse. He'd mumbled incoherently when she hooked him up to the portable oxygen supply, but not since. She thought she heard him mutter her name, then admonished herself for grasping at straws.

"What medical steps were taken in the field?" her father asked, inserting IV needles into the backs of each man's hand.

Freddy told them.

Slamming two Insta-Cold packs on top of a cooler to activate them, Aubrey laid one on Gage's forehead and the other on Marty's, who kept refusing to lie still.

She passed him some water and instructed, "Sips only. I mean it." Using a sports bottle with a spout, she dribbled water into Gage's mouth.

He licked his lips and croaked a raspy, "Thank you."

Though she knew he was hardly out of the woods, her hopes nonetheless flared.

While her father saw to Marty, Aubrey took Gage's temperature, which was elevated, and tended to his many abrasions. Later, when he was more responsive, she'd check his eyes and flush them with saline solution if necessary. For now, she gently sponged them with cool water.

He talked in broken sentences, mostly about the fire. He made more sense than earlier but far from perfect sense. Bit by bit his body temperature decreased, and bit by bit his mind cleared.

When she was done, she sponged his chest with a washcloth and mild cleanser. Beginning at his neck, she made small circles, frequently rewetting the washcloth in a basin of water and squeezing on a fresh dab of cleanser.

Aubrey didn't hurry. She knew every inch of Gage's torso—having explored it on numerous occasions with her hands and mouth—and treated it to a thorough bathing. His arms and hands received the same careful attention.

Medicine wasn't the only method of treating the sick and injured. A loving touch also healed. With each stroke and caress, she willed Gage to recover, her fingertips communicating more effectively than any spoken word.

Lost in her task and oblivious of her surroundings, she leaned down and dropped a kiss on his chest, right over the place where his heart beat, strong and steady.

When she lifted her head and looked at his face, she nearly came unglued.

Through puffy eyelids, he watched her, his gaze focused and the corners of his mouth curling in a crooked grin. "You're here," he said in a gravelly whisper. "I thought I was dreaming."

She gave a small gasp.

His grin drooped. "Do I look that bad?"

"You look awful," she wailed and wrapped her arms around his neck, pressing her cheek to his.

Hissing, he flinched.

Aubrey immediately drew back, realizing she'd mistakenly irritated his abraded cheek. "Oh, gosh. I di—"

"S'all right. His grin returned, still crooked and impossibly sexy. "My mouth doesn't hurt."

"Good." She kissed him soundly, careful to cup only the left side of his face.

He reeked of smoke, sweat and gasoline, but he tasted like heaven on Earth and felt like forever and ever.

His arm came up and encircled her waist. Held her. Cherished her. When they separated, Aubrey was crying.

"Do you have any stomach cramps?" she blubbered.

"No." He chuckled. "Is that why you're crying?"

She shook her head and sniffed. "I'm crying because I said some terrible things to you the other night, and I'm sorry. So, so sorry."

"Shh, baby." He lifted his hand and rubbed his knuckle along her jawline. "Don't apologize."

"I was wrong."

"We were both wrong. And both right." He stared at her with undisguised hope. "Since you're still hanging around, maybe we can talk later."

"We're going to do a lot more than talk."

"Oh, yeah?" His tone was low and suggestive. "Like what?"

She guessed he was thinking of his old motor home and how they might go there and "talk" like the day he'd burned his hand. Little did he know she had something far different in store for them.

When precisely she'd made up her mind, Aubrey wasn't sure. It might have been when she saw Gage being lowered from the engine, or when he carried her sick grandmother into the house. For all she knew, it was the day they ran into each other at the convenience store, and this moment had been coming for the last six weeks. Pinpointing the exact second her life changed was irrelevant. Aubrey loved Gage and couldn't—*wouldn't*—leave him. Ever.

She sat up straight, steeled her resolve and blurted, "Like get married."

"Are you proposing?" He shot up, or tried to shoot up, and got only as far as leveraging an elbow on the cot before Aubrey placed a restraining hand on him.

"Yeah, I am." Brushing aside the last of her tears, she busied herself by checking his IV, intensely cognizant of everyone else in the tent watching them. "Any headache? Dizziness?"

"No and no. Aubrey, I—"

"Nausea?"

"Damn it, Aubrey!"

Freddy, who was still standing at the head of Gage's cot holding the IV bag, didn't bother to hide his amusement. Aubrey ignored him, along with the three other people sharing the tent who were also enjoying the show.

"Stop fussing for one lousy minute, will you?" Gage snapped.

She did stop fussing, and their gazes connected. So, it seemed to Aubrey, did their souls.

"You sure you want to marry me?" he asked. "Really sure? No running back to Tucson this time. Once you're wearing that ring, you're stuck with me for good." As if to emphasize his point, he found her hand and folded it inside his.

"I'm sure." She could hear the absolute certainty in her voice, and it pleased her. Bending down to kiss him again, she discovered yet another manner in which touch healed.

"I love you," she murmured against his lips. "I have since I was four years old. And for the record, I don't want to date long distance, and I don't want to just live together."

"Me, either."

"Not so fast." She placed a finger on his lips when he would have sealed their engagement with another kiss. "I expect the whole nine yards this time."

"Meaning?"

"Diamond ring, long white dress and a romantic honeymoon in some fabulous, far-off locale." She sighed, remembering the photograph of her grandparents. "San Francisco."

Gage angled his head and said to Freddy, "Is it just me, or is she being bossy again?"

"Take my advice, *amigo*. Agree with whatever she says. You'll stay married a lot longer this time." When his buddies broke into raucous laughter, Freddy made a face. "What? Am I wrong?"

"Men." Aubrey harrumphed and took Gage's temperature, glad to see it was nearly normal.

Suddenly serious, Gage asked, "What about your job? And the promotion?"

"I'm considering a career change."

"Since when? And to what?"

"Since I started working with my dad." She turned toward her father and beamed. "I'm going back to school to become a physician's assistant."

"That's great," Gage said.

"Yeah, it is great."

Her father winked at her, and Aubrey sensed the many pieces of her life coming together.

Leaving Marty's side, her father came over to stand beside her. He stroked her hair, the gesture a familiar one that harkened back to when she was a little girl. "I'd ask how our patient's faring, but it appears to me like you have everything under control." He extended his hand to Gage. "I guess congratulations are in order."

Gage didn't hesitate and returned the handshake.

"You're a fine man, Gage. What you did today took courage. Your family will be very proud of you."

"Thank you, sir."

Her father nodded before releasing Gage's hand. "Don't you think it's time you called me Alex, considering you're about to become my son-in-law? Again."

"Past time, Alex."

Kissing the top of Aubrey's head, he commented, "Your mother will be overjoyed. She's been planning your and Annie's weddings for years."

Aubrey rolled her eyes, imagining the commotion her mother would soon be generating. "I'd forgotten about that."

Every head turned when the tent flaps opened, and a tall, authoritative man squeezed into the tent.

The firefighters holding the IVs snapped to attention. Gage attempted to rise.

Before Aubrey could restrain him, the man said, "Relax, Raintree." He approached the cot, his hand extended. "Ms. Stuart?"

"Yes?" She stood and accepted his handshake.

"I'm Commander Newcombe. Thank you for coming."

"Happy to, sir. And this is my father, Dr. Alexander Stuart. He came with me."

"I heard we had a famous heart surgeon on board." Commander Newcombe went over to the other cot and shook Aubrey's father's hand. "We're honored and grateful for your help, as well. How are our patients?" His glance traveled from Marty to Gage.

"They're going to be fine," Aubrey answered.

"I'll be back on the line as soon as I can stand." Digging his heels into the cot, Gage tried to rise. He didn't get far.

"You're not going anywhere for the next twenty-four hours, except to the infirmary at Fire Camp," Aubrey interjected.

"You listen to the young lady," the commander warned. "She knows what she's talking about."

"Hey, I've been telling him the same thing," Freddy chimed in.

Gage grumbled. "The fire will spread to our ranch if it's not stopped."

"One of the tankers radioed in a few minutes ago," the commander said. "The backfire your men set and the line you dug is holding."

Gage didn't look convinced, but neither did he defy doctor's orders, rip out his IV and make a run for it.

"You're to be commended, Captain," the commander told Marty. "You and your crew leader." He turned to Gage. "You have a real future ahead of you, Raintree. Have you ever considered making firefighting a full-time career?"

"I have. Often."

"Excellent. We can always use good instructors and administrators. Come see me when you're ready."

"Yes, sir."

"Oh, I almost forgot. I have a message from your family. We've been in contact with them because of the fire's proximity to your ranch."

"A message?"

"Your mother sends her love and says not to worry about them. Take care of yourself."

Gage smiled, and Aubrey thought it was just like Susan to put her son's safety ahead of her own.

"And your father wishes you well."

"My father?"

"Yes." The commander quirked one eyebrow. "I believe his exact words were 'good luck'."

"Well, I'll be damned." Gage shook his head.

Aubrey reached down and put a hand on his shoulder. She didn't want to read too much into the two words, but maybe—hopefully—Joseph Raintree was beginning to come around.

She walked the commander to the tent flap. "Do you suppose the fire will be contained soon?"

"Hard to say. But my guess is the worst is behind us."

Aubrey pulled the tent flap aside and peered out. Flames could be seen sprouting from the tops of distant trees, and smoke climbed in billowy columns to the sky.

"May I inquire how long you're going be in Blue Ridge?"

She grinned broadly. "A while."

Another year and a half, at least. Once she and Hannah both finished school, then Aubrey and Gage would move to Pineville. Or not. She could always run the clinic.

"Can we count on your help during the next fire?" Commander Newcombe asked.

"You can." Wherever she and Gage lived, she'd continue working part-time as a wilderness medic for the Forest Service.

He saluted her, then ducked and went outside. Aubrey returned to tend to her patients. Happiness filled her at the sight of Gage and her father, the two men she cared most about in the world, talking amiably and no longer at odds.

The whine of a distant siren sounded. Faint at first, it increased in volume.

"Gentlemen," Aubrey's father announced, "your limo has arrived."

Aubrey grabbed one of the portable stretchers.

"No!" Gage's objection halted her in midstep. "I may have been carried in here but I'm walking out."

"You're too sick and weak." Her protest had no effect on Gage, especially since Marty, with the help of her father, was already standing.

"Fine." She huffed. "Then let me help you."

Gage relented with a shrug. "If it involves your arms around me, then okay."

She and Freddy managed to hoist Gage to his feet but it was a struggle. They shuffled across the tent with Freddy on one side of Gage, holding the IV, and Aubrey on the other, holding the portable oxygen tank.

"Do I get to come to your wedding?" Freddy asked.

"Sure." Gage grunted. "You can even be one of my groomsmen."

"All right!"

Maneuvering the tent opening required considerable effort. Gage was out of breath and sweating profusely when they finally emerged on the other side where the EMTs waited.

"Ride with me?" Gage asked Aubrey.

"I…should…probably stay. In case there are more injured." She wanted desperately to accompany him in the ambulance but duty called.

"Go," her father said. "I'll hold down the fort and drive your car home later."

"Really?"

"Yes, really. And don't forget to call your mother."

She blew him a kiss before crawling into the back of the ambulance after the EMTs had loaded Gage. The last thing she saw through the rear window of the ambulance as it pulled away was her father clapping Freddy on the back.

Then, looking down at Gage, she saw the rest of her life stretched out before her.

"You know where I want to go when this is over?" he mumbled as the EMTs took his and Marty's vitals.

"The motor home?"

"There, too." He had trouble keeping his eyes open. "I was thinking of the creek. We can celebrate."

Aubrey smoothed a damp lock of hair from his face. After ten years, she had everything she wanted—could have *always* had, only she'd been too stubborn and too afraid to realize what really mattered in life. Not where she lived or what job she held, but being with Gage.

"I'd like that," she murmured and pressed a kiss to his forehead.

After all, they had a lot to celebrate, and their secret spot was the ideal place.

* * * * *

THE ROYAL HOUSE OF NIROLI
Always passionate, always proud

The richest royal family in the world—
united by blood and passion,
torn apart by deceit and desire

Nestled in the azure blue of the Mediterranean Sea, the majestic island of Niroli has prospered for centuries. The Fierezza men have worn the crown with passion and pride since ancient times. But now, as the king's health declines, and his two sons have been tragically killed, the crown is in jeopardy.

The clock is ticking—a new heir must be found before the king is forced to abdicate. By royal decree the internationally scattered members of the Fierezza family are summoned to claim their destiny. But any person who takes the throne must do so according to The Rules of the Royal House of Niroli. Soon, secrets and rivalries emerge as the descendents of this ancient royal line vie for position and power. Only a true Fierezza can become ruler—a person dedicated to their country, their people…and their eternal love!

*Each month starting in July 2007,
Harlequin Presents is delighted to bring you
an exciting installment from*
THE ROYAL HOUSE OF NIROLI,
*in which you can follow the epic search
for the true Nirolian king.
Eight heirs, eight romances, eight fantastic stories!*

Here's your chance to enjoy a sneak preview of the first book delivered to you by royal decree…

Five minutes later she was standing immobile in front of the study's window, her original purpose of coming in forgotten, as she stared in shocked horror at the envelope she was holding. Waves of heat followed by icy chill surged through her body. She could hardly see the address now through her blurred vision, but the crest on its left-hand front corner stood out, its *royal* crest, followed by the address: *HRH Prince Marco of Niroli…*

She didn't hear Marco's key in the apartment door, she didn't even hear him calling out her name. Her shock was so great that nothing could penetrate it. It encased her in a kind of bubble, which only concentrated the torment of what she was suffering and branded it on her brain so that it could never be forgotten. It was only finally pierced by the sudden opening of the study door as Marco walked in.

"Welcome home, *Your Highness*. I suppose I ought to curtsy." She waited, praying that he would laugh and tell her that she had got it all wrong, that the envelope she was holding, addressing him as Prince Marco of Niroli, was some silly mistake. But like a tiny candle flame shivering vulnerably in the dark, her hope trembled fearfully. And then the look in Marco's eyes extinguished it as cruelly as a hand placed callously over a dying person's face to stem their last breath.

"Give that to me," he demanded, taking the envelope from her.

"It's too late, Marco," Emily told him brokenly. "I know the truth now…." She dug her teeth in her lower lip to try to force back her own pain.

"You had no right to go through my desk," Marco shot back at her furiously, full of loathing at being caught off guard and forced into a position in which he was in the wrong, making him determined to find something he could accuse Emily of. "I trusted you…."

Emily could hardly believe what she was hearing. "No, you didn't trust me, Marco, and you didn't trust me because you knew that I couldn't trust you. And you knew that because you're a liar, and liars don't trust people because they know that they themselves cannot be trusted." She not only felt sick, she also felt as though she could hardly breathe. "You are Prince Marco of Niroli…. How could you not tell me who you are and still live with me as intimately as we have lived together?" she demanded brokenly.

"Stop being so ridiculously dramatic," Marco demanded fiercely. "You are making too much of the situation."

"Too much?" Emily almost screamed the words at him. "When were you going to tell me, Marco? Perhaps you just planned to walk away without telling me anything? After all, what do my feelings matter to you?"

"Of course they matter." Marco stopped her sharply. "And it was in part to protect them, and you, that I decided not to inform you when my grandfather first announced that he intended to step down from the throne and hand it on to me."

"To protect me?" Emily nearly choked on her fury. "Hand on the throne? No wonder you told me when you first took me to bed that all you wanted was sex. You *knew* that was the only kind of relationship there could ever be between us! You *knew* that one day you would be Niroli's king. No doubt you are expected to marry a princess. Is she picked out for you already, your *royal* bride?"

* * * * *

Look for
THE FUTURE KING'S PREGNANT MISTRESS
by Penny Jordan
in July 2007,
from Harlequin Presents,
available wherever books are sold.

HARLEQUIN®

Mediterranean
N I G H T S™

Experience the glamour and elegance of cruising the
high seas with a new 12-book series....

MEDITERRANEAN NIGHTS

Coming in July 2007...

SCENT OF A WOMAN

by

Joanne Rock

When Danielle Chevalier is invited to an exclusive
conference aboard *Alexandra's Dream,* she knows it
will mean good things for her struggling fragrance
company. But her dreams get a setback when she
meets Adam Burns, a representative from a large
American conglomerate.

Danielle is charmed by the brusque American—
until she finds out he means to compete with her bid
for the opportunity that will save her family business!

www.eHarlequin.com   HM38961

Do you know
a real-life heroine?

Nominate her for the Harlequin More Than Words award.

Each year Harlequin Enterprises honors five ordinary women for their extraordinary commitment to their community.

Each recipient of the Harlequin More Than Words award receives a $10,000 donation from Harlequin to advance the work of her chosen charity. And five of Harlequin's most acclaimed authors donate their time and creative talents to writing a novella inspired by the award recipients. The More Than Words anthology is published annually in October and all proceeds benefit causes of concern to women.

HARLEQUIN

More Than Words™

**For more details or to nominate
a woman you know please visit**

www.HarlequinMoreThanWords.com

MTW2007

nocturne™

**DON'T MISS THE RIVETING CONCLUSION
TO THE RAINTREE TRILOGY**

RAINTREE: SANCTUARY

by *New York Times* bestselling author

BEVERLY
BARTON

Mercy, guardian of the Raintree
homeplace, takes a stand against
the Ansara wizards to battle for
the Clan's future.

*On sale July,
wherever books are sold.*

SNRT2

THE GARRISONS

A brand-new family saga begins with

THE CEO'S SCANDALOUS AFFAIR

BY ROXANNE ST. CLAIRE

Eldest son Parker Garrison is preoccupied running his Miami hotel empire and dealing with his recently deceased father's secret second family. Since he has little time to date, taking his superefficient assistant to a charity event should have been a simple plan. Until passion takes them beyond business.

Don't miss any of the six exciting titles in **THE GARRISONS** continuity, beginning in July. Only from Silhouette Desire.

THE CEO'S SCANDALOUS AFFAIR

#1807

Available July 2007.

Visit Silhouette Books at www.eHarlequin.com   SD76807

REQUEST YOUR FREE BOOKS!
2 FREE NOVELS PLUS 2
FREE GIFTS!

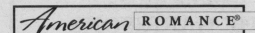

Heart, Home & Happiness!

YES! Please send me 2 FREE Harlequin American Romance® novels and my 2 FREE gifts. After receiving them, if I don't wish to receive any more books, I can return the shipping statement marked "cancel." If I don't cancel, I will receive 4 brand-new novels every month and be billed just $4.24 per book in the U.S., or $4.99 per book in Canada, plus 25¢ shipping and handling per book and applicable taxes, if any*. That's a savings of close to 15% off the cover price! I understand that accepting the 2 free books and gifts places me under no obligation to buy anything. I can always return a shipment and cancel at any time. Even if I never buy another book from Harlequin, the two free books and gifts are mine to keep forever.   154 HDN EEZK   354 HDN EEZV

Name _____ (PLEASE PRINT) _____

Address _____ Apt. # _____

City _____ State/Prov. _____ Zip/Postal Code _____

Signature (if under 18, a parent or guardian must sign)

Mail to the **Harlequin Reader Service®**:
IN U.S.A.: P.O. Box 1867, Buffalo, NY 14240-1867
IN CANADA: P.O. Box 609, Fort Erie, Ontario L2A 5X3

Not valid to current Harlequin American Romance subscribers.

Want to try two free books from another line?
Call 1-800-873-8635 or visit www.morefreebooks.com.

* Terms and prices subject to change without notice. NY residents add applicable sales tax. Canadian residents will be charged applicable provincial taxes and GST. This offer is limited to one order per household. All orders subject to approval. Credit or debit balances in a customer's account(s) may be offset by any other outstanding balance owed by or to the customer. Please allow 4 to 6 weeks for delivery.

Your Privacy: Harlequin is committed to protecting your privacy. Our Privacy Policy is available online at www.eHarlequin.com or upon request from the Reader Service. From time to time we make our lists of customers available to reputable firms who may have a product or service of interest to you. If you would prefer we not share your name and address, please check here. ☐